Rousing the Duvelsbeest

by Nils Visser

Illustrated by Tom Brown, Julieann Williams, & Julie Gorringe

Rousing the Duvelsbeest, 2025.

Paperback ISBN 978-1-8382427-6-3
eBook ISBN 978-1-8382427-7-0
Cider Brandy Scribblers
Brighton, Sussex, England
Text copyright © 2025 **Nils Visser**
Front Cover Illustration **Tom Brown**
Back Cover Illustration **Julie Gorringe**
Interior Illustrations: **Tom Brown, Julieann Williams, &
Julie Gorringe**

Instructions for use: Start at the beginning and read all the words one after the other until you come to the very end and then stop.

Dedicated to the memory of
David Thomas Kellie

Contents

Foreword

1. Bloody Hard Yakka

2. Running the Easting Down

3. Camp Whoop Whoop

4. Tempestuous Welcome

5. Fragments

6. The German Girl

7. Osteoarchaeological Revelations

8. An Extraordinary Encounter

9. Bipedal Oddities

10. Savages

11. *Ay Baya* !

12. Might is Right

13. Extant & Edible?

14. Suitably Contrite

15. A Heartfelt One to One

16. Moonlit Promises

17. Birds of a Feather

18. At the Mercy of Brutes

19. An Exercise in Insanity

20. *Was Zum Teufel*?

21. Lost and Found

22. Gory Banquet

23. Liselotte's Journal

24. Grim Work

25. Oh *Mi Gado*

26. A Promise to Fulfil

27. The Usual Suspects

28. *De Blokzeyl*

29. Stickybeaked Sandgropers

Acknowledgements

Foreword

The island of Arenes, on the Australian west coast, appears on a world map only once, in 1550. Are subsequent omissions a peculiar oversight by cartographers? Or might it be that the island simply doesn't want to be found? Arenes certainly has sound reasons for such a preference...

Although this story takes place on an island that may or may not exist, it relies on a wider Australian context and references the mainland. I would like to acknowledge the traditional owners of that land and pay my respects to their elders, past and present.

I've used archaeology, not Indigenous histories, as reference for some aspects of this story but they do appear in oral histories and rock art, and this is duly acknowledged. I have used respect for one's natural environment as a core theme as I sincerely believe people from all nations would benefit by walking the talk.

To this I need to add an apology to the Western Australian Museum for I have shamelessly borrowed from your exploits. Please know that I stand in awe of your remarkable achievements in the field of maritime archaeology.

Brighton, January 2025

1. Bloody Hard Yakka

Arenes, Western Australia, 2016

Lette Sabajo reminded herself, not for the first time since they'd set out from Maroons Cove, that she was lucky to be here. The reminder was necessary because her current discomfort wasn't exactly something she associated with luck.

The single road that ran across the heart of Arenes Island – through an endless vista of dry shrubs and low stunted trees – merited the designation 'road' only because the uneven dirt track was the sole way to reach the island's rugged west coast by car.

The road had long exacted a toll on the four-wheel-drive's suspension. The vehicle shuddered, juddered, bounced, and bolted along at a top speed of twenty miles an hour on straight stretches. Slower when it had to manage bends and inclines or negotiate gullies and dry creek beds. A cloud of red dust drifted in the four-wheel-drive's wake but also persisted in penetrating the supposedly sealed interior. Lette's nostrils were slowly clogging up with fine dust and it settled on her tongue whenever she opened her mouth, though that at least could be washed away with a sip from her water bottle. Her khaki trousers and beige long-sleeved blouse were gradually discolouring, blending into a singular reddish hue as if she were being claimed by Arenes. The vehicle's airco was struggling in a losing battle with the heat. Although Lette much preferred to perspire like a lady if she had no other choice, she was sweating profusely, stains darkening her blouse at the armpits, back, and underside of her boobs.

Lucky indeed.

Back in Amsterdam she had been pleasantly surprised that she had been selected for this assignment. At a mere twenty-eight she was a relatively junior member of staff at the National Maritime Museum. Her only claims to fame were her efforts as an intern to digitalize the museum's extensive archives and participation in wreck dives in Sussex, England. The last to explore Dutch ships that had been sunk during the Battle of Beachy Head in 1690, often scuttled on purpose to avoid capture by the victorious French navy. She had fond memories of those dives. Peering through the dusty windows at the monotone of the landscape outside, she couldn't help but recall with some nostalgia the evenings by the hearth fires of quaint English pubs tucked into folds of the South Downs as they discussed the day's dive over a pint of beer.

Her current ordeal in the dry dustiness of Arenes had started with a brief message from Australia that had caused a considerable buzz in the hallways and offices of the National Maritime Museum.

New wreck discovered, likely VOC.[1] *Archival expertise appreciated.*

Normally, Lette and her colleagues tended to become a bit possessive when it came to VOC wrecks. Those had

---

[1] Abbreviation for the Dutch East Indies Company.

been Dutch ships after all. The English especially excelled at museumsplaining Dutch ships to Dutch experts. It was well intentioned but always conveyed the notion that continental European cognitive abilities were primitive at best and required English leadership and direction to achieve full potential.

This message, however, had hailed from the Maritime Archaeology Department of the Western Australian Museum in Fremantle. These were the guys and gals who had been involved in the exploration of the wrecks of *De Batavia*, *De Zuytdorp*, *De Zeewijk*, and *De Vergulde Draeck*.

And possibly some English ships, Lette thought with a wry grin. *But those fade in comparison with the VOC wrecks.* Those dives, the divers involved, and the risks taken in hazardous conditions were legendary in the world of maritime archaeology.

It was typical of the Western Australians to contact their colleagues in Amsterdam to ask for help in verifying that this new wreck was a VOC one. The professional courtesy was much appreciated but if the Western Australian Museum said it was likely to be a VOC wreck, then there was no doubt in Amsterdam that they would be correct. The Aussies had more than earned their spurs in this field. The big question would be which particular ship – there were no obvious candidates – and the Australians had long learned that Dutch assistance in deciphering Dutch language archives could save them a lot of headaches.

If this new wreck compared to the famous four, anyone sent out from Amsterdam could add a major coup to their career. There'd likely be a book in it, lecture tours, that sort of thing. Lette had figured that her seniors would be forming a double queue for the privilege, but to her surprise many hadn't translated their enthusiasm into practical steps to obtain the prize. Some of the older ones had told her that they had made their names, were now orientated towards retirement, and figured it was time for a new generation to step up. Some had smirked and Lette reckoned that they didn't fancy eating dust on Arenes, being far more aware than she had been as to what discomforts would be involved. Quite possibly the museum's director had nailed it when he'd told her that few other staff members had her extensive knowledge of the archives. However, she'd been partially formed by Dutch culture, so Lette was cautiously modest about her own abilities and therefore more likely to suspect ulterior motives on behalf of others rather than admitting to herself that she was damn good at her job and deserved this assignment.

She patted the rectangular bag that she held clutched to her side as if it were a pirate's treasure. The bag contained, among other things, the laptop to which she'd transferred much of the digital archival materials. She had been forewarned that there was no Wi-Fi on Arenes. She took out her mobile phone and switched it on to verify once again that she had no signal. The last time she had a signal was when she'd left Geraldton – on the mainland coast – aboard the boat that was to take her to Arenes. It was strange to conclude that her phone, a usually continual connection to the world – her parents, her fiancée Marvin –

had been reduced to a shiny and useless bauble, although she supposed she might be able to snap a few pictures with it.

Lette focused on the view afforded by the dusty window again, only to conclude that the perpetual endlessness of the semi-arid landscape hadn't changed a bit.

Arenes Island was about ninety miles long and fifty miles wide. It was located a hundred and twenty-two nautical miles west of Kalbarri National Park, on a northwest bearing from Geraldton. The island had first appeared on Pierre Desceliers's 1550 world map but had simply disappeared from maps since then, or more recently been portrayed as an area to be avoided because of the treacherous reefs that surrounded most of the island. The reason for the island's long omission was quite possibly because there wasn't much here. Most of the island consisted of an escarpment rising from the sea to support a massive plateau covered with low and dry vegetation. Any green hues the shrubs and trees might have possessed were dulled by the red dust. She had been informed that rainfall, common out here on the ocean during the winter season, would transform the vegetation into vivid greens, as well as filling in the many water holes that pockmarked the plateau on a regular basis.

The towering cliffs along the long western coast and the shorter northern and southern coasts offered a handful of small, sheltered coves but no safe anchorages for anything larger than a launch. The plain on top of the escarpment, though not quite flat, held no defining landmarks, other than a low ridge of higher terrain that separated the escarpment from a narrow stretch of low coastline on the east coast. That lowland was defined by a few streams of fresh water that wound their way into marshy mangroves.

The island had been surveyed in the sixties and seventies but nothing of value had been found. There was no coal, oil, natural gas, iron ore, bauxite, diamonds, gold, silver, zinc, nickel, lead, copper, platinum, palladium, manganese, tungsten, opals, phosphates, sapphires, or topaz to excite industrial interest. There was plenty of dolomite, but that was common enough elsewhere in Australia where it was much more economically viable to exploit. The main natural resource was to be found along the stretch of eastern coastline, between the mangroves and the extensive reef barriers, where there was good fishing to be done. This industry supported the island's only township, Maroons Cove, so named because local legend had it that centuries ago VOC ship captains had found it a suitably convenient and desolate place to maroon crew members found guilty of serious misconduct.

Maroons Cove wasn't a pretty place, a collection of prefabricated shacks inhabited by rough and stoic fishermen who preferred to mind their own business. More than half the population was temporary, present for the peak fishing season from April to August and then returning to the mainland. No tourists visited the island. Although it had docking facilities these were aimed at fishing and not suitable or attractive for the yachting community who much preferred places like Albany,

Bunbury, Mandurah, Fremantle, or Exmouth. With an abundance of men and almost no women or children, Maroons Cove exuded the sort of atmosphere that Lette associated with America's Wild West. She had been informed that when the township's two pubs shut this was almost always accompanied by a few drunken fistfights. These usually involved arguments about fishing rights or outrageous boasts about the day's catch that beggared belief to such an extent that it was deemed offensive and merited a few corrective whacks.

Lette's attention turned to her driver, a young man who was rather incongruously called Bruce.

Lette herself was rather tired of introducing herself as being Dutch at international gatherings and having to harvest the inevitable comments about wooden shoes, tulips, and windmills. She would struggle to smile like a farmer with a toothache (as the Dutch say) because she had been raised to be polite. The truth was, she was a city girl who considered herself to be cosmopolitan. She had never worn wooden shoes in her life, wasn't particularly fond of tulips – she much preferred peonies, amaryllises, lilies, and hyacinths –, and all she knew about windmills was that they looked pretty as a backdrop in the green flatlands when she traveled from one city to another.

Much worse was when she identified as a Dutch woman and this wouldn't be accepted by other Dutch folk – the white-skinned variety.

"But where are you really from?" some would persist.

"Amsterdam," Lette would answer. "Born and bred."

Schooled as well, surrounded by Dutch culture during her formative years.

"Yes, but where are you *really* from?"

Lette would feign ignorance. If they persisted this long they were conveying their notion that a black person couldn't possibly be Dutch but simply had to hail from elsewhere. In that case, they were the ones who would have to formulate their own prejudices. She'd be damned if she'd do it for them.

Many settled for, "where are your parents from?"

"Surinam," Lette would then answer, finding this question somewhat more acceptable, though it still conveyed the notion that she didn't really belong in the country where she'd been born and raised.

"Ah, so you like roti and saoto soup?"

Lette would have to struggle to avoid rolling her eyes. Of course she liked roti, what sane person didn't? But she also liked pancakes or *poffertjes* [2], could easily wolf down a whole pack of *drop* [3], or contemplate murder for a *stroopwafel* [4].

Sometimes she couldn't restrain herself and would bare her teeth. "My family likes to stuff plump Dutchmen into a huge cooking pot and boil them alive while we bang on drums and dance in front of our palm huts."

The other would then leave, muttering about the woke sensitivity of ethnic minorities. They never got the message

---

[2] *Poffertjes* - Battercakes, a type of Dutch small fluffy pancake served with butter and icing sugar.
[3] *Drop* - Dutch liquorice.
[4] *Stroopwafel* – a Dutch caramel waffle.

that she was mirroring their own expectations, but at the very least it was satisfying to air her annoyance.

Since flying into Perth, Lette had discovered that many Australians seemed to relish their national identity, wearing stereotypical elements like a badge of pride. Had anyone back in the Netherlands told her that she would be awaited in Maroons Cove by a bare-chested, tanned, young man with a wide grin called Bruce, she would have accused them of watching too much Monty Python. But Bruce was called Bruce and acted like a Bruce. He also spoke like a Bruce, with a flat, nasal twang which Lette suspected he exaggerated for her benefit. That in combination with the slang – which she also suspected was exaggerated – made it hard for her to understand him at times, though she supposed she'd get used to it.

Apparently aware of her contemplation of him, Bruce uttered another string of nonsense. "It's bloody hard yakka, this, but at least we won't have to chuck a uey on this road, hey? Only one place it goes and that's out whoop whoop."

"*Ja*," Lette agreed, refusing to ask for clarification. "We must be getting closer now?"

"Reckon! Now if them bludgers haven't put on their cozzies to sunbake all arvo, they'll be ready to chuck a snag and a chook on the barbie and we can bog in right off!"

He looked at her expectantly. Lette suspected that he hoped she would betray how much he'd managed to confound her, but Bruce clearly didn't know that stubbornness was a Dutch trait. She wasn't planning to surrender to his gobbledygook that easily.

She muttered, "*Yu de mi wan meti.*"[5]

"Say again?" Bruce asked, looking puzzled.

"Sorry, I slipped into Creole." Lette grinned. "I could use a beer after this drive."

"A bey-ah! Good onya." He responded enthusiastically. "We got those, it ain't a BYO[6], we even got them cold."

He continued to happily expound about beer and Lette was glad they had found a topic of common interest to discuss.

She studied his driving with admiration. He wasn't so much guiding the vehicle like one would on a Dutch road, as engaged in a life and death battle for control over the four-wheel-drive on a road that seemed to have a mind of its own. Bruce clamped the steering wheel in a death grip – both wheel and hands vibrating continuously – and had to apply considerable pressure when turning slightly to the left or right. When they had to slow down to maneuver down into a gully his legs would work the pedals frantically.

"Sorry about the wheels, by the way," Bruce said. "They expect us to work miracles, but when we ask for some moolah to make that possible the message is always that there are no dollarydoos."

Able to make sense of that, Lette informed him, "Same as us. We're meant to keep the public proud of our heritage but every time they can they cut our budget some more."

---

[5] Sranantongo (Sranan), the informal language of Surinam. Literally this phrase means: 'You are a piece of meat', which means as much as 'You're quite something, aren't you?' used in a derogatory manner.
[6] Bring Your Own

"Well lookie there," Bruce said. "We've arrived! Camp Whoop Whoop. See them mounds? Those hold the caves where we found evidence of wreck survivors."

Lette stretched her neck to take in low flat-topped mounds ahead, beyond which the land simply disappeared. She supposed that's where the escarpment ended, with steep cliffs dropping down to the Indian Ocean. There was a camp to the left of the largest mounds, multiple colourful tents of all sizes and a few trailers.

All notions of discomfort were gone in an instant. There was work to be done here, a puzzle to be pieced together. The mention of survivors sent a thrill through her as well. To think that fellow Dutchmen had been here hundreds of years ago, in dire circumstances at the edge of the world, was breathtaking.

In contrast to her own imminent arrival, however, those countrymen hadn't got here by traveling across the plateau. They had come from the other side. From the ocean, having sailed eleven thousand nautical miles to get here, where they most certainly didn't want to be.

2. Running the Easting Down

The Brouwer Route (Roaring Forties), Indian Ocean, 1616

A landlubber would have called it a stormy eve. A seaman would have defined the weather as a mite iffy.

Leyn Jonas had spent months at sea since setting sail from Flushing Roadstead in Zeeland, as ship's boy on the East Indiaman that was struggling with the obstinate ocean. Landlubber no more, but he still lacked the swagger and confidence of most of his crewmates in the focsle.

When he stepped outside onto the rain-swept foredeck he kept his opinion on the elements – *fuck this weather* – to himself. Using expletives was asking for trouble, the kind that involved the boatswain's lash. He'd learned that particular lesson ere they had even cleared the English Channel.

Leyn was tall for his sixteen years, with a mop of unkempt fair hair that fell over his ears and to the nape of his neck, and some optimistic fluff on his chin and cheeks. He was barefoot, wearing brown woolen breeches and a once-white linen shirt. Both garments were threadbare and much patched. His only other attire consisted of a large red handkerchief tied around his neck and a wool hat.

Leyn clutched the gunwale for support. The deck pitched this way and that, moving at the whim of the towering waves. It was on the cusp of the evening, but he couldn't see far beyond the ship – other than a turmoil of water and sky.

He took stock of the ship. Or at least the parts of the ship he could see from the foredeck. The spritsail and jibs were furled, as were the topsails on the foremast and mainmast. Only the foresail and the mainsail were in action – he couldn't see the mizzen. The sails were reefed to keep the wind from ripping them off the masts: spars, rigging, and all.

Leyn decided that the weather was more than a bit iffy. It was wearing him down. More than six hours of nothing but the howling wind, pounding waves, drumming rain, briny spray, tense orders, and apprehension had turned life into never-ending misery. Worse, it would get dark in a few hours and the heavens showed no signs of abating their fury.

A thunderous voice filled Leyn's ears. It belonged to Boatswain Rykert. "Leyn Jonas! Your mess bain't summoned topside! Why the Devil are you on deck?"

Leyn turned to face the boatswain, an ill-tempered giant of a Hollander from Alkmaar. The bridge of Rykert's nose had been flattened in a long-forgotten fistfight. A scar ran diagonally from the tip of his left eyebrow to the right corner of his stubbled chin, giving him a permanent sneer. His eyes were a mean brownish-yellow. The boatswain was notoriously sharp of sight, devilishly quick to note transgressions by ship's boys.

Leyn had to shout to be heard over the waves, wind, and rain. "I have to use the head, Boatswain. I have to shit."

Rykert regarded Leyn with disdain. "You came up for a shit? In this weather? You bain't got much of a brain. That be normal for a Zeelander, but none-the-less…"

Leyn squirmed. He had to go so badly that he was prepared to grovel and beg. "Please, Boatswain. I really need to go."

Rykert nodded at the head. "Well then, don't let me stop you. What are you waiting for?"

Leyn scurried forward to the head. The seating plank, with a gaping hole in the middle, extended over the hull near the bowsprit. He unfastened his breeches, nearly tumbled over when the ship pitched sharply to larboard and then held on to the rigging for dear life – even as he gave way to the pressure that had been building up in his bowels.

Rykert stepped up to the gunwale, to look at the turmoil caused by frothing waves and fierce winds. He hollered conversationally, "Full broadside! You really did need to go Jonas. But you're a daft fool."

"Aye-aye, Boatswain. A daft fool." Leyn shouted back, feeling awkward. He had got used to the lack of privacy on the head but still didn't like it. Shitting, he reckoned, was private business.

Leyn hoisted up the old rope that dangled next to the seating platform. Its frayed end, washed by the sea, was purposed to conclude this particular activity.

Rykert continued. "The lads make use of a few buckets down in the focsle in this weather. A lot more sensible than risk becoming shark food."

He hollered conversationally, "Full broadside! You really did need to go Jonas."

(Illustration by Julie Gorringe)

Leyn hesitated but found the courage to share an observation. "Aye, but the crew empty the buckets down the orlop hatches."

"If you try to carry a full bucket topside in this breeze you'll get covered in shite. Come to think of it, that might be an improvement in your case."

Leyn rose, hoisting up his breeches. His vacated bowels were a source of relief. "But the orlop deck is where the soldiers live."

Rykert grinned. It wasn't a pretty sight as it twisted his already disfigured face horrendously. "That's the fun part."

The seamen and soldiers on board hated each other with passion, but some of the soldiers had families down below. Leyn had watched them when he could, during their daily one-hour stint on the weather deck. Fathers, mothers, and children. Leyn himself had grown up in an orphanage. His crewmates might see folk from the orlop as vermin, but to Leyn the sight of a family was a treasure to behold — even when pale, shaky on their legs, and gasping for fresh air. Certainly not something to pour both scorn and shit upon.

He wasn't going to admit such soppy sentiments to Rykert though. The boatswain was being uncharacteristically kind but might not be so inclined if he sensed softness to be mocked.

Leyn frowned when he glanced at Rykert's face. The boatswain was staring out into the murky remnants of daylight, a helpless expression on his face, his usually predatory eyes filled with fear.

"By God's gonads! May the almighty Lord have mercy on our souls."

Leyn followed his frit gaze. The boy's mouth fell open.

Another ship. A strange type, with an outlandishly designed hull that was grey with age and much battered. Her once proud but now tattered colours – red, white, and blue – showed she was a fellow Dutchman. None of her torn and frayed red sails were shortened or furled, all billowing out fully…as the strange ship sailed straight into the wind.

Leyn did a double take, but there was no doubt about it. The ship's sails curved outward – head into the wind.

Leyn cried out "But... but… that's not even possible!"

The ship was making full speed – impervious to the raging elements – and merged with the gloom beyond the East Indiaman's stern.

Rykert asked Leyn, "Did you see her?"

Leyn nodded, still stunned by the impossibility. "But it can't be? Was that thing real?"

"It be bad luck to speak her name. She were lost years ago. Running the easting down along the Roaring Forties, just as we are doing now. The ship was last seen sailing into a cyclone between the Isle of Arenes and the landmass of New Holland. They say that sighting her brings ill fortune."

"But...you're scared of her!" Leyn blurted out – utterly astonished that this tarred and salted giant, this bane of ship's boys, could be afraid of anything. It was as unbelievable as a ship sailing head into the wind. Realizing that his words merited a punitive thump about the head, Leyn quickly added, "Begging your pardon, Boatswain."

The boatswain seemed oblivious to Leyn's transgression, shaking his head with worry. "Not frit of the ship so much, Jonas, as of the waters she sails on. We must be much farther east than the skipper calculated and in dire danger. I must warn the officers. You stay here. Keep a look-out."

"A look-out for what?" Leyn asked, but Rykert had already hurried aft.

Leyn went as far forward as he dared, folding an arm around the bowsprit for support. He peered through the sprit shrouds at the tempestuous waters below, then at the murky gloom ahead – hearing the wind howl and waves roar. The foul weather continued to limit visibility. The strange ship had disappeared to their stern, what did Rykert think was to their bow?

Leyn was distracted by a rasping voice. One that was all too familiar and not at all welcome.

"Hell's bells! I spot a shrimp-dick on deck."

Leyn turned reluctantly to face Govert Bastiaansz. The sailor, dressed akin to Leyn, was in his late twenties. His weathered and pockmarked face was ever tense with fury, suggesting pent-up violence within. Bastiaansz was a bully who liked to torment ship's boys when out of sight of those who applied the ship's strict disciplinary measures.

Leyn had good reason to both hate and fear Bastiaansz. The sailor generally didn't mind much which ship's boy he targeted, but he had taken a special interest in making life miserable for two of Leyn's friends, Koos and Jurian, both a year younger than Leyn. Koos and Jurian had found solace and strength in each other's company, which in turn had led to them finding comfort in each other's arms.

This wasn't unusual between males on a ship during a long voyage. It wasn't allowed, of course, but as long as it was kept discreet the customary reaction of other crew members was to ignore it altogether. Not so Bastiaansz. Infuriated by the inner strength Koos and Jurian inspired in each other, which prevented Bastiaansz from breaking their spirits, he had made a point of seeking the boys out and catching them in the act.

Then Bastiaansz had raised the alarum, notifying the ship's officers that the sin of sodomy had taken place and was likely to call God's wrath on both ship and crew. At that point the outcome was irreversible, spelled out in detail in the Company's disciplinary provisions. Koos and Jurian had been placed back-to-back on the weather deck, tightly bound together by a great many lengths of heavy chains. When the skipper had read the ship council's verdict Koos had cried and pleaded for mercy, whilst Jurian had stared ahead of him in silent defiance.

The crew had been summoned to witness the punishment, most of them with sullen resignation as the boys had generally been popular. All knew that they had been driven together out of self-preservation against the incessant bullying they had been subjected to. Of course, Bastiaansz and his cronies had not been sullen or silent. They had taunted the condemned boys – Bastiaansz with barely concealed triumph – and cheered when the bound Koos and Jurian had been shoved overboard to be drowned in the ocean for their sins.

Leyn didn't care much what Koos and Jurian had or hadn't done. That had been their business, not his. What he did know was that he'd counted both boys as his friends. Koos's tears, Jurian's defiance, Bastiaansz's triumphant sneers, and Koos's panicked scream of terror when the lads had been cast overboard would be etched on Leyn's soul until the day he died.

Leyn regarded Bastiaansz warily now, fully aware that the bully wasn't just vicious but potentially lethal. He tried to think of a reply that would allow him to stand his ground without triggering Bastiaansz into an explosion of hostility.

Before he could think of one, his world was turned upside down.

Things happened in bewildering succession.

A splintering crash below his feet.

Knocked onto the deck.

An upward lift as the East Indiaman became airborne.

Very briefly.

She crashed back down with a thunderous thud.

The keel shrieked as it broke on impact.

Leyn was hurled off the bow and plunged into the dark sea

Another ship. A strange type, with an outlandishly designed hull that was grey with age and much battered.

(Illustration by Tom Brown)

3. Camp Whoop Whoop

Arenes, Western Australia, 2016

When Lette stepped out of the dusty four-wheel-drive she was welcomed by an elderly gent who peered at her through his spectacles beneath wild unkempt silver eyebrows that gave him an owlish look.

"Miss Sabajo, I presume," he said amiably. "I'm Martin Fieldman, Director of Operations here in Camp Whoop Whoop."

"Pleased to meet you, Mr Fieldman. So the camp is really called Camp Whoop Whoop? Bruce said so, but…"

Fieldman threw an accusatory glance at Bruce, who stepped forward with a grin.

"Did Bruce let on that he speaks English? Or did he put on his Jackaroo act?"

"Jackaroo? Me?" Bruce asked with indignation.

Fieldman ignored him, turning his attention back to Lette. "He's got a few roos[7] loose in the top paddock. We've developed a theory here at Whoop Whoop that Saint Nick must have presented Bruce with a copy of an Aussie slang and phrase book as Chrissie prez one year, and that dear old Bruce has only ever read this one book."

"Not fair," Bruce protested. "I'll have you know that I've also read *Possum Magic* and *Strong Little Platypus*[8]."

---

[7] Roo is slang for kangaroo
[8] Australian children's books

Ignoring him again, Fieldman continued, "Meaning he can be a bit of a drongo at times, but he's our best bush driver and only the best will suffice for you, Miss Sabajo, as we hope you will be able to help us answer some questions about our find."

"I will do my best, Mr Fieldman," Lette promised.

"Please call me Martin," Fieldman suggested. "Bruce, would you mind taking Miss Sabajo's luggage to her assigned tent? I'll show our esteemed visitor around."

"Will do, Mr Bossman," Bruce agreed.

"Lette, please, Martin," Lette said.

"Lette it is. Wreck site, caves, finds? What would you like to see first?"

"Wreck site," Lette answered immediately.

"Very well," Fieldman agreed. "Though mostly we'll be having a squiz at what you can't see."

They walked through the camp, drawing a few curious glances but most people were far too concentrated on various tasks to pay them too much attention. Whereas a first look at the camp had conveyed a merry chaos, closer inspection revealed some sort of order. Bruce had parked the four-wheel-drive at a rectangular area cleared of rocks with about a dozen other vehicles parked on it, all four-wheel-drives. This makeshift car park formed the outer limit of the camp. There were a few windowless transport containers lining it that Lette assumed served as storage facilities. A generator growled away in an open shack.

To their left, well away from the generator, was a disorganised scattering of smaller tents or bungalow tents, placed haphazardly around rocks and boulders. Lette assumed that these were the sleeping quarters. Next to that, closer to the centre, was a large marquee with long tables and camping chairs, as well as an extensive field kitchen. There was a wide path between this catering quarter and what appeared to be the more official part of the camp, three huge rectangular army-green tents flanked by smaller ones with opened sides to reveal desks and cabinets. One of the latter sported an array of antennae and exuded the garbled chatter of a field radio.

"Our connection to the outer world," Fieldman nodded in the direction of the radio tent. "We can talk to Maroons Cove, our boat, and on a good day even Geraldton."

"And the three big tents?"

"Go by the very scientific names of Landlubber's HQ, Sea Dog's Cabin, and the Morgue."

"Land finds, dive finds…and bodies? Have you recovered remnants?"

Fieldman nodded, with a grim expression. "Plenty. I'll show you later."

They walked out of the camp and came to a ledge where the land sloped down for sixty or seventy meters at a fifteen-degree angle before ending abruptly. Lette came to a halt, gasping at the sight of the Indian Ocean stretching endlessly to the north, south, and west. Even from their vantage point, at least fifty meters above the sea level, Lette could discern the great size of the swelling waves that rolled toward Arenes with relentless force.

"Quite a view," Fieldman said. "If you look to your right, you can see the cave entrances in the mounds."

Lette looked and saw gaping vertical slashes in the mounds. Almost the entire seaward looking flanks of the mounds were open faced, and within rose natural stone columns as if they were temples of old. She could also see a few trenches in front of the larger caves in which archaeologists appeared hard at work.

"The two largest ones were used by the wreck survivors," Fieldman explained. "Obviously, we've built our camp well way from them so as not to contaminate the ground around them."

"How many people have you got on site?" Lette asked.

"About two score and a few more. All sworn to secrecy. We're on a good wicket here, so trying to keep the find a secret for as long as we can, to keep the vultures away."

Lette nodded, recalling how much damage had been done at previous wreck sites that had drawn treasure seekers from far and wide. Some had even used dynamite on reefs to enable easier access to artefacts.

Fieldman started walking down the slope. "We won't go all the way down today, Lette. Just to the edge of the scree slope. All we'll achieve by going further down is to get soaking wet as it's high tide and then face an exhausting climb back up."

His words made sense to Lette when they reached the edge of the slope. To either side of them the cliffs rose over the ocean at a near vertical angle, exuding surly menace. Between the two sets of cliffs, however, like a breach in an old medieval city wall, was a slope consisting of scree and boulders, steep indeed but just about accessible.

"The scree is a devil to get up and down," Fieldman explained. "It'll shift at times which means a much faster descent that you counted on, or else sliding you back down when you're trying to get up."

At the base of the scree slope was an uneven platform of sorts, made of coral reef with boulders of different sizes scattered around. The waves shattered against the edge of the platform, sending showers of spray erupting upward and over the platform. Occasionally a geyser-like eruption of water would burst up from holes in the platform.

Lette observed those columns of water. "Blowholes? So, it's an undercut reef?"

"Indeed. Making diving extremely hazardous, while at the same time holding the alluring promise that many materials may have been swept beneath the platform."

"The diving is weather dependent then?" Lette asked, even though the answer was obvious.

"We need the calmest of weather, and even then, it's hazardous. We've managed a few preliminary dives to map things out but haven't brought much up yet. Many of the finds in the Sea Dog's Cabin are from the shoreline platform or the bottom of the scree slope, rather than from the ocean's clutches."

"What have you discovered about the ship's demise?"

"See those rock formations to the left of the platform? We've identified two large anchors there, which has led us to believe that's where the ship ran into the reef.

We think with sufficient force to break the bow clean off. We've identified a great many of the cannon, you see, and they're not behind the bow section. Instead…"

He swept his hand to the right, along the shoreline platform. "The cannons are scattered parallel to the platform. Remnants of masts as well."

"So, the main part of the hull was swept sideways by the ocean," Lette mused, trying to envisage the scene in front of her. "Have you found a port and starboard pattern to the cannons?"

"No. It's not an exact straight line, of course, but all the cannon we have found are placed in an uneven but single row, many of them on top of others. Proper dog's breakfast."

"She capsized then?"

"That's the working assumption. We need a few good diving days to explore that theory, map out the *in situ* layout in more detail and then bring up the first finds. The lads are all for raising a few cannons, as you may imagine."

"Cannons may have useful inscriptions," Lette agreed. "But my preference would be…there." She pointed toward the right of the shoreline platform.

"The stern," Fieldman said.

"If your assumption is correct that's where the stern would be. And within the stern…"

"The coin chests."

"Coins would be useful for dating and that would help a great deal in identifying this ship. Unless you've found or located the ship's bell?"

Fieldman shook his head. "Not as of yet."

"The VOC lost about 675 ships. We can whittle down that list by excluding those that are known to be lost on the Atlantic, or in the Indies, and those of which the wrecks have been located. But that still leaves hundreds of which the last known location was 'somewhere' on the Indian Ocean."

Fieldman let out a low whistle. "Talk about a needle in a haystack."

"A firm date, even a rough date would potentially bring down the number to a dozen potential candidates…or less if we're lucky."

Lette let her eyes roam along the shoreline platform. Her mind's eye was able to at least envisage some of the scene. The ship ploughing into the reef. Limited visibility then? Evening, nightfall, or driven by the madness of a cyclone. The main part of the hull pushed sideways by the waves. What would it have been like for those belowdecks? Eating or bantering in their mess, maybe swinging in a hammock. The shock of the impact would have sent everything and everyone flying. A flood of cascading water from the torn bow. Then a mad rush to the deck to escape the water. A deck that was about to become vertical as the ship capsized.

A shiver ran down her spine as Lette watched the waves explode onto the reef. It would have been mayhem and carnage down there. Sheer terror. An unpredictable lottery of random death.

It was irrational to feel helpless, she knew. There was little she could change about an unfortunate event that had taken place hundreds of years ago. There was something she could do, though, to honour the life and death struggle that had taken place down below. To honour the dead. That was to identify the ship, mayhap name some of those whose hopes of reaching Batavia had perished upon that ocean-battered reef.

She whispered, "who are you?"

4. Tempestuous Welcome

Arenes, The Southland, 1616

The turmoil of the howling winds disappeared when Leyn was plunged beneath the sea. The clamour of the waves became a constant but muted rumble. The death cries of the East Indiaman were audible.

My ship, Leyn thought. *My poor ship.*

He could hear her broken keel grinding against rock, as if both were viciously sawing into each other. He faintly registered from within the hull the sound of two hundred people screaming, wailing, and cursing.

Leyn had rolled himself into a ball when he hit the waves. Now he was tumbled around until he no longer knew which way was up. He panicked, started kicking his legs frantically and propelled himself into a direction that could just as well be up or sideways — or straight down.

That realisation increased his panic, but the ocean wasn't done with him yet. He was sucked up into the surge of a giant wave that lifted him up and then spat him out.

Leyn didn't land in a wet embrace again, instead crashing hard onto porous dead coral rock with razor sharp edges. Instant pain screamed through his body. All his bones seemed to have been jarred loose by the force of the impact. Vicious stings criss-crossed his skin as if he had been lashed all at once by a hundred boatswains.

Dazed, Leyn scrambled up, nearly fell, and then sank on his knees, trying to understand what was happening a mere stone's throw in front of him.

The East Indiaman's bow was wedged into the reef the ship had ploughed into, but the gigantic incoming waves were pressing the stern to larboard, forcing the ship to make a turn that was accompanied by the splintering of ribs and strakes at the bow.

The doomed ship's decks were filling with people. Leyn could see the soldiers' wives and children, milling on the weather deck, close to the forecastle. The officers on the quarterdeck were moving their mouths as if bellowing orders, but their voices were overpowered by the chilling screams of hundreds of people staring death in the eyes. A few folks along the gunwales caught sight of Leyn. By their expressions he knew that they considered him fortunate, although that did little to remedy the vicious pain on his arms and legs from the bite marks of the coral's teeth.

Leyn's mouth dropped open as he beheld a mountainous wave gathering height, rising over the East Indiaman with deadly grace. The slow climb of the wave was countered by its speed when it fell, tons of water thumping the stricken ship. The humongous swell at the wave's base pushed at the East Indiaman. The bow was torn loose from the rest of the ship. The opened hull began to take in large quantities of water at once, even as it rolled sideways.

Around two score people managed to cling on to rigging. Leyn reckoned they were sailors.

The rest ululated a collective shriek that overpowered waves and wind as folk lost their balance and started to slide down the decks. Their legs were kicking out and their arms scrambling about in an instinctive but vain search for support. The first people who thudded against the gunwales were soon lost from sight as more and more piled on. Folk began to tumble over the mass of writhing bodies crushed against the gunwales, straight into the turmoil of the dark sea.

The horror Leyn felt at the plight of those aboard the East Indiaman was added to by renewed danger. The ship's sideward roll swung her masts down. The spars of the topsails came hurling at the reef like giant spears.

Ignoring his pains, Leyn scrambled to his feet and rushed backward, away from the murderous spars, the ends of which disintegrated on impact with the reef and sent a shower of splinters flying about. The shrieking on the East Indiaman ended abruptly as all and sundry on the decks were swept off the decks to be swallowed by the voracious sea.

Those in the rigging had started scrambling to the ends of the masts hanging over the reef. Leyn recognised the formidable shape of Rykert in the main mast's shrouds. The men began to drop off, onto the solid ground below. A few howled in pain as they twisted or broke ankles and legs.

A dozen or so didn't make it. The East Indiaman began to rise again, lifting those left on the shrouds and rigging in the air. Ere the ship could become fully upright she was slammed by more incoming waves, broke apart, and sank altogether. The bow had been bucking the reef, a few folks holding on for dear life, but now disintegrated into loose wreckage that was thrown about like unwanted toys.

Cries for help and screams of pain between the sinking remnants of the ship competed with the thunder of Rykert's voice.

"Get those people out of the water! Now!"

Those who could, about two-dozen sailors and Leyn, made to the edge of the reef to be met by a desperate sight.

The ocean's waves raged, sweeping in to explode against the rocks and then surging out again. Amidst floating debris from the ship – and far too many lifeless bodies – were frantic people, clawing at the water or clutching on to larger pieces of wreckage. Some shouted for help, others howled their pain. Some were picked up by the waves and smashed against the sharp edges of the reef, shrieking as their skin was shredded.

Those who survived that punishment and managed to cling on to the reef found helping hands and were pulled up to safety. In the water, many of the living flailing about the debris saw this and tried to make it to the reef. They entered a morbid lottery. Not all could swim, or do so very well, and they were the first to be swallowed by the waves. Some, bleeding profusely, managed to scramble up, but others had bones or skulls shattered when they were smashed against the reef, or were cut so badly that their struggles weakened until they sank below the frothing water. At least one potential rescuee pulled his would-be saviour down into the turbulent waters, condemning both to a briny grave.

Leyn lost track of the time – his own pains momentarily forgotten – as he filled his lungs to holler encouragement at desperate swimmers and took hold of outstretched hands. The last person he helped up was a dark-haired girl his own age – one of the orlop folk – who clung to him sobbing. Bereft of energy, Leyn sank down to console her, finding it soothed his own horror.

"This way! This way!" some of the sailors shouted at the wild waters, but the scores of remaining bodies were unresponsive, lifelessly tossed about by the triumphant ocean.

Another mountainous wave rolled in to explode against the reef, spitting spray and wreckage at those who had made it ashore.

Rykert boomed, "We are too exposed. Move inland."

Leyn turned his head to look away from the ocean. As far as he could make out, they were at the base of dark cliffs that rose high, though there was a nearby breach that seemed to offer a steep passage up.

The boatswain led a score of sailors up the scree slope to scout. This vanguard consisted of the sailors who had clung to the rigging and made it to the reef with minor scratches at most. About sixty survivors followed, forming a ragged column. None of these seemed to have escaped the ship's destruction unscathed. Those with minor injuries supported the more severely injured. Leyn wasn't pleased to see Govert Bastiaansz and some of his cronies amid the pitiful procession.

A handful of folks remained on the narrow wave-swept base of the cliffs – cut by coral so badly that they had bled to death in the short time between flopping onto the shore and the survivors' retreat from the ocean.

Leyn and the girl formed the rearguard.

"What happened?" The girl asked in confusion, slowly emerging from shock and taking in her surroundings.

She spoke with a German accent. Many of the soldiers from the orlop came from there. All down on their luck to such an extent that they had volunteered to serve in the East, destined to garrison a climate rich in insidious fevers, hostile warriors, and hungry critters large and small.

"We hit a reef."

"Is this all that's left?" There was disbelief in the girl's voice as she beheld the struggling survivors in front of them.

Leyn feared that it might be but fervently hoped that mayhap others had somehow landed on a different stretch of reef. If not, that meant that more than one hundred and forty souls had departed this world in the space of minutes. Too many for him to comprehend. Images of those he had watched die replayed in his mind's eye. He pushed them away.

"I don't know."

"Where are we?"

"I don't know that either."

"You don't know much, do you?"

Leyn considered the girl's question for a moment, as they negotiated a boulder resting on the scree. He answered honestly, "Nay, I don't know much at all."

The girl made a noise that might have been a pained laugh. She was struggling. She was only wearing a simple white shift, and her bare legs had been cut badly.

"I'm Heike, Heike Steenbeck."

"My name is Leyn Jonas."

They concentrated on the next stretch of scree. It was hard going and agony on bare feet. The precarious stuff gave way every now and then, making it hard to retain their balance.

What Leyn had thought to be the tops of the cliffs were a false summit. The ground rose further, mildly sloping up another sixty meters. There was vegetation here, low brush struggling to survive on the rocky underground. Silhouetted against the murky sky were what appeared to be rectangular structures with flat tops.

Buildings of sorts?

Relief washed through Leyn as he reckoned these shapes indicated human habitation…shelter, food, drink, and the welcome warmth of a fire. The end of the worst of this ordeal, surely.

Some of Rykert's vanguard stood by the side of the largest rectangular structure, waving the ragged column of survivors toward them. When they came closer to the formation, Leyn registered with disappointment that it was a natural mound rather than a man-made building.

Walking was easier on the mild slope, but Heike increasingly leaned on Leyn for support, so progress was slow, and they were the last to arrive.

5. Fragments

Arenes, Western Australia, 2016

Lette indicated the shoreline platform; "I can't imagine this is a place where divers would come for a bit of leisure time, nor even a random hiker making their way down the scree for the sheer fun of it. So, I assume you located the wreck after finding…"

"The caves," Fieldman answered promptly. "Come, I'll show you."

Climbing up the moderate slope toward the largest of the caves, he explained. "There was a fellow from Maroons Cove who drove a lady friend out here. You've done the drive, might seem a bit farfetched for a picnic and some, ahem, privacy."

Lette grinned. "I can imagine that a change of scenery from Maroons Cove might be appreciated, as well as solitude away from town. Especially by the romantically inclined."

"Indeed. Anyhow, they noticed that the cave's ceiling was blackened by soot. Not just in a spot or two, which might indicate an occasional fire built by folks like themselves, but all over, indicating a great many fires, possibly over a longer period of time."

As they approached the flat-topped mound with its wide-mouthed cave entrance Lette reasoned that if she were a shipwreck survivor, climbing the escarpment to get away from the ferocious waves and grim scenes of death, that cave would be a most welcome sight. She would have certainly made a beeline toward it.

Fieldman produced a small flashlight from a pocket and turned it on to light their way.

The cave's ceiling was low enough to force Lette to crouch as they entered the cave, but the cave was extensive, made mazelike by the many columns, with chambers reaching deep into the mound and the ceiling rising again within. Instead of the rocky soil outside, the floor inside consisted of soft dark grey sand. It didn't take much imagination for Lette to conclude that if you were exhausted, in shock, and possibly injured, the notion of curling up on the soft sand was preferable to the uncomfortable ground outside.

Fieldman shone the light over the ceiling that was indeed soot stained.

"The woman was an acquaintance of one of our colleagues back in Fremantle and notified us as to what they had found. We sent out a small field team to investigate, thinking that maybe we had at long last found evidence of human habitation on Arenes."

"Are there Indigenous people on Arenes?"

"No, no records of them and no traces were ever found. Which made a field trip worthwhile. It would have been a significant discovery, to be sure. There's not much out there, as you have seen, so it was feasible that a structure like this, with all the columns, would have had a special significance to any Indigenous people who might have lived here in the past. What we found, however…" He shook his head. "It might be better to show you in the Landlubber's HQ."

"Lead the way," Lette agreed.

When they re-entered the camp, she noted a distinct difference in fashion. Most of the crew were dressed in miniscule shorts, the smaller the better seemed to be the maxim, with the men bare-chested and the women wearing skimpy halter tops. They all had magnificent tans and walked about entirely unconcerned by the sun's relentless glare. A minority, however, were pale, or painfully red, and wore loose trousers that covered the entirety of their legs and long-sleeved shirts or blouses, as well as floppy hats and sunglasses. They limited their time in the sun, darting from shaded area to shaded area with all the characteristics of prey trying to evade some winged predator.

"How many Dutch people work in the camp?" Lette asked Fieldman.

"About half-a-dozen," he answered. "How did you..." He looked around him and then grinned. "There's always a contingent of Dutch folk on the west coast these days. Interns or post-grads. We believe they make a valuable contribution. And Professor Penning, of course."

"Karin Penning? Is she here?"

Before Fieldman could answer, the heavy flap of the tent that served as Landlubber's HQ was lifted and an elderly woman strode out. Her fair hair was greying and tied back in a girlish ponytail. The wrinkles on her face suggested that she could swerve from mirth to sternness in an instance. She wore a similar outfit to the other Dutch crew, but her wide-brimmed hat was a straw one and she also wore a pink silk scarf, lending her the glamorous appearance of an old-fashioned movie star. Lette recognised her immediately. Professor Karin Penning was a giant in her field. She was mostly a resident of Western Australia these days, but on the occasions that she visited Amsterdam Lette had always signed up for her lectures on the famous four, the Australian VOC wrecks that had yielded enough information to provide work for a lifetime as Penning was fond of saying. Lette wasn't particularly religious, but if she had been Karin Penning would have featured prominently as a primary goddess in the pantheon.

"Dying for a smoke," Penning informed Fieldman, proceeding to light up. Her eyes fell on Lette. "You must be Miss Sabajo, fresh from the Dam?"

"Professor Penning!" Lette exclaimed. "It is an honour to meet you. I've read all your…"

"*Ja, ja, ja*," Penning said impatiently, capturing Lette in an intense stare. "But did you bring *drop*, girl? Did you bring *drop*?"

Having been forewarned that proper Dutch liquorice was as good as gold with any Dutch folk she might meet out in Oz, Lette nodded. She reached into her satchel and retrieved a random packet of *drop*, of the salty triangular variety.

Penning's eyes widened and her haughty demeanour changed into that of a needy supplicant. "You're an angel sent from heaven, Miss Sabajo."

Lette handed over the packet that Penning took with reverence, carefully tearing it open to avoid spilling any of the content. With childlike glee this academic giant, author of a thousand papers and harsh taskmaster of scores of undergraduates, popped a piece of liquorice into her mouth and made infantile noises of joy.

"What's this then?" Fieldman plucked a piece from the open bag and flicked it into his mouth. His expression changed into one of disgust almost immediately and he spat it out. "Crikey, that's feral!"

Both Penning and Lette looked at him in horrified astonishment. One did NOT, on no account, casually spit out a piece of *drop*. It was unheard of.

"Philistine," Penning muttered. "Savage!" She bent over to pick up the piece of *drop* and tried in vain to brush off the sand. Then she slid the protective plastic cover off her pack of cigarettes and deposited the *drop* in it. "That will wash off under some water."

"That's been in my mouth!" It was Fieldman's turn to be astonished. "Surely you're not going to eat it."

"It's *drop!*" Professor Penning and Lette voiced simultaneously, then looked at each other and smiled.

"We'll get along just fine," Penning promised Lette. "Has this barbarian descendant of convicts come to show you my treasures?"

"Technically, they're the museum's," Fieldman mumbled.

"As I said, 'my' treasures," Penning said sternly. She extinguished her cigarette and pressed the butt in Fieldman's hand. "Be a dear and get rid of that for me, and I might, *might*, forgive you for mistreating my *drop*. Come inside, Miss Sabajo."

"Lette will do," Lette said quickly, delighted at being in Penning's good graces.

"I would prefer 'Your Eminence," Penning grumbled. "But HR won't have it. Apparently, I have to settle for Professor."

Apart from a tea corner, the large tent was lined by long tables on which individually labelled items were laid out with care, rank upon rank of them like they had turned out for an army parade.

"Have you seen the caves?" Penning asked.

"Just the largest one," Lette answered, itching to get closer to the finds.

"For some reason the survivors used two caves. It might be that there were many more than we first assumed if that large cave was overcrowded. It's that long table there; those are all finds from the larger cave. The first field team started finding artifacts the instant they started sifting through the sand."

Lette wandered over and took in the items with wide eyes. There were bottles, whole and broken, wine glasses, tin plates, jars, pots, spoons, knives, musket balls, buttons, barrel hoops, and broken clay pipes. Some of the jars and plates were clearly marked with the VOC logo.

"No coins though," Lette mumbled.

"More's the pity," Penning agreed. "But it's early days yet. Come and take a closer look at this."

The professor indicated a pistol that had a rusty barrel but a grip and stock that were in remarkably good condition for wood. A small copper plate still bore the VOC logo.

"A wheel lock!" Lette exclaimed. "Must have been an officer's, those were expensive."

"Indeed," Penning agreed. "And unless it's an heirloom of sorts, it gives an indication as to the age of the wreck."

Lette nodded. "It pretty much rules out the 18th century, even the latter half of the 17th century. Some of these musket balls..." Lette sounded puzzled.

"You know the drill. Gloves if you want to handle them." Penning indicated a box of surgical gloves on the table, and it was only then that Lette noted these boxes were spread about on all the tables between the finds. She slipped on a pair and began to pick up some of the musket balls to examine them more closely. They were made of lead, and some of them had distinctly flattened sides with raised jagged edges like miniature volcanic craters.

"Some of these have been fired, struck hard objects."

"Like cave walls," Penning nodded. "It looks like they had troubles."

Lette carefully placed the last musket ball she had picked up back on the table, murmuring to herself, "The VOC was founded in 1602, so any earlier date that might be indicated by the wheel lock is ruled out by use of the VOC logo – unless that copper plate was a later addition? The wheel lock was used into the 17th century, but gradually replaced by the doglock and flintlock, so my guess would be 1602 to 1650, maybe 1660..."

Struck by a memory, Lette glanced at the tea corner. "Professor, would you mind if I set up my laptop there?"

"Had a brainfart?" Penning asked. "Be my guest. As a matter of fact, has that liquorice spitter offered you a cup of tea yet? Nay? Director of Operations indeed, tut tut. I'll make you a cup while you beaver away. In exchange I'll claim all the credit for any amazing discoveries you make. They have to be amazing though, mind you, I won't settle for mundane now, do you hear me?"

Penning chattered away but Lette shut out her voice as she removed the surgical gloves, opened her laptop and started it up.

An initial 'Arenes' search yielded nothing except a few references to onboard trials that had resulted in the island being named as a place to maroon offenders, at least lending weight to the origins of the name of Maroons Cove.

She was sure, however, that she had previously encountered the name of Arenes elsewhere.

Fragments! That's a separate file altogether.

Not all records survived the march of time unscathed. Even the vellum often used instead of parchment on board of ships to ensure greater durability could be vulnerable to the wet and damp conditions during a journey, not to mention clumsy accidents or fire. As an intern Lette had insisted on compiling a digital collection of fragments. Their value as historical documents were often considered dubious, missing the wider context of what document or time period the fragment hailed from, and relaying incomplete information at best. However, Lette believed that incomplete information of dubious origin was better than no data at all.

Fieldman had wandered into the Landlubber's HQ and gratefully accepted the offer of a cup of tea from the professor. He and Penning were discussing the weather forecast for the next day, which had come in by radio from Geraldton, as well as the promise of an extreme low tide that they spoke of with hopeful anticipation, when Lette looked up at them.

"I may have found something."

Fieldman and Penning immediately crowded around the laptop.

"I'm not sure," Lette said, made nervous by their full attention, feeling her comparative lack of experience weighing heavily upon her shoulders. "But this is from a fragment of a Dutch document archived by the Bahari Museum in Jakarta. It's dreadfully incomplete but makes mention of a shipwreck on Arenes."

> *Ten years ago in the year of our Lord 16…*
> *…VOC ship De B…*
> *…Skipper Ha…*
> *…hove to in sight of Arenes…*
> *… met by an astonishing sight…*
> *… from the VOC ship De…*
> *…struck a reef and was wrecked…*
> *…loss of all her cargo and 193 souls…*

Penning translated for Fieldman. "Trust the VOC to focus on the loss of cargo before the loss of human life."

"It could be our ship," Fieldman mused.

"Unless there are more wrecks on Arenes," Penning agreed. "Which would also be interesting."

"I'm wondering how this ship the 'Bee' and Skipper 'Ha' knew that 193 people died," Lette mused. "If he saw what was left of the wreck, he could have deduced that she'd struck the reef, and if there was no cargo other than the odd jetsam and flotsam of the type you've found in the caves, the loss of cargo too would be a logical deduction. But 193 is a fairly specific number."

"You're on to something there, Lette," Fieldman mused. "Might they have found a muster roll? A log that also kept track of the usual deaths en route to allow a calculation of living crew when she struck the reef?"

"If the captain of our ship had had the time to stuff his logs and papers in waterproof bag, perhaps," Penning said. "Gathering his papers would have been standard procedure in an emergency. But would he have had the time? From what we can surmise – the ship's course indicating that no evasive measures were taken – they had little to no warning and the immediate urgency of the calamity would have been pressing. Moreover, those bags were weighed down with lead as the purpose was to sink sensitive information to prevent it from falling into hostile hands, not to merrily float about until located by God-knows-who. I think it's more likely that this Skipper 'Ha' would have heard it first hand from survivors."

"So, it's possible the 'Bee' picked up survivors," Lette said. "There might be a record of that somewhere. It would have certainly been logged."

"I'm a bit surprised, to be honest," Fieldman confessed.

"Why?" Lette asked. "Doesn't the occupancy of two caves indicate a great many survivors?"

"Someone had to bury them, Martin," Penning noted.

"Yes Karin, but that might have been done by the outlying bodies…"

"Bury? Outlying bodies?" Lette asked, confused.

Fieldman assumed that grim expression she'd seen earlier when she'd inquired about possible human remains. "You'd best come and look."

Penning nodded. "Time to visit the Morgue."

6. The German Girl

Arenes, The Southland, 1616

Despite his weariness and the shock that still stunned him, as well as disappointment that the rectangular structures weren't man-made habitats, the sight of a long cave burrowed into the mound astonished Leyn. Its entire seaward flank lay open, and all around this wide entrance – as well as deeper within – were columns of stone rising to the ceiling in a stately manner, as if in a church or temple. The cave was filled with survivors. Rykert was hollering multiple commands at once to establish some order.

"Jopie, take a dozen men down again and get hold of anything useful from the ship. Be careful down there though, what with the waves hurling wreckage ashore. Jonas, glad you could join us. You did good work on the reef. Well done."

Leyn was flabbergasted, thinking, *I did? Did he really just say that?*

The boatswain continued his litany of orders. "Floris, take two men and mount a guard atop the cave. Send someone down if you see anything. Nelis, Willem, you and the rest help Niklas. Jonas, join them."

Leyn was pleased to see that the ship's surgeon, known simply as Niklas, had survived and was organising the wounded into different groups. Niklas was an old salt, tall and broad-shouldered like Rykert but grizzled and grey.

The surgeon had always been kind to Leyn, but frowned when he took in the sight of Heike clinging on to the ship's boy. "Oh dear, here comes trouble."

"Is she hurt badly?" Leyn asked, worried that he had underestimated the severity of Heike's injuries.

"The problem is 'she'," Niklas clarified. When he saw that Leyn didn't understand, he added, "I admire your naivety, Leyn. Best get her to that far corner, over there. Out of sight if you will."

Leyn supported Heike to the indicated corner, where two women in their thirties from the orlop lay on the ground, cut as badly as Heike was.

Leyn carefully helped Heike down. The ground consisted mostly of dark sand, a soft contrast to the scree and rocky ground outside.

"*Danke*[9], Leyn."

"You're safe now."

Heike frowned. "*Das ist totaler quatsch!*[10] Didn't you hear the surgeon?"

"Aye, he told me to bring you here."

She rolled her eyes and shook her head for a reason Leyn couldn't fathom. He recalled seeing the girl before.

"You're from the orlop, aren't you? You were with that young soldier, in the red breeches."

"*Ja…mein bruder*[11]…Bertram…"

---

[9] *Danke* – German for 'thanks'

[10] *Das ist totaler quatsch* – German for 'That's complete nonsense'

[11] *Mein bruder* – German for my brother

The sudden grief that struck her face made Leyn keep his mouth shut. He had no idea what words could be spoken to soothe such a stark loss.

Heike shivered uncontrollably for a moment. "We made our way to the weather deck together. We managed to stay together in the water, in that horrible sea. He was hurt badly, smashed up against that reef. The last thing he did was push me up. Up to you."

"Oh."

One of the women studied Heike with a combination of disbelief and fragile hope. "Heike? Heike! *Wirklich?*[12] Is it you, Heike?"

The two exchanged rapid bursts of German, then held each other and sobbed.

Leyn rose to his feet, uncertain what to do next. The cave was filled with people, some walking among the many who were reclined – moaning and groaning – on the sand. Leyn recognised Jacob Dirksz, another one of the ship's boys, leaning against the cave's back wall, a gash on his forehead. He had his arms around a young boy and a young girl – around six or seven years old – who were clearly distraught. All the other survivors were men. The only other females were in Leyn's corner, and apart from Jacob's two wards there were no children to be seen.

There were at least a dozen kids in the orlop.

Nor did Leyn see any others from the East Indiaman's complement of a score of ship's boys. He couldn't see any

---

[12] *Wirklich* - German for 'really?'

of the ship's senior officers either, leaving Rykert and Niklas in charge.

Leyn shivered, struck by a sense of enormous loss.

The first salvaged goods from the ship were brought up. Casks of water and bread were deposited at Rykert's feet.

"The tide is still coming in Boatswain. Covering the reef and washing stuff up. Plenty more to be salvaged."

"Go, Jopie. Go and get it. Everything you can."

Niklas summoned Leyn. He handed him two small casks. "Water and bread. For your corner. Give them a few sips of water first, everyone will be thirsty."

"And then feed them bread?" Leyn guessed.

Niklas shook his wizened head. "Add some water and chew the bread, Leyn, until it's soft. Then smear the pulp on the worst of the cuts."

"Stick chewed bread on wounds? Really?"

"Chewed bread. It will have to suffice until I have something else to work with. Now get chewing. I have broken bones to set. Willem, get Jacob and the children to Leyn's corner."

Willem Duyt, the sailor addressed by Niklas, ushered Jacob and the two children after Leyn as he returned to the women in his corner.

"Where are my *mutti* and *vati*?[13]" one of the children asked between sobs. "I want my *mutti*."

---

[13] *Mutti* and *vati* – German for mummy and daddy

The two older women in the corner each took a child in their embrace, murmuring to the sobbing children in German.

The patients in the corner were grateful for sips of the water. Heike watched Leyn break off a bit of the bread he had fished from the bread cask.

"Can I have some of that bread?" she asked hopefully.

"It's not for eating, just now." Leyn examined the bread. It was hard as rock. He tapped it against the side of the cask to encourage the weevils within to depart.

He could hear Niklas hollering from another part of the cave, shouting at the two sailors assisting him. "Hold him down!"

That was followed by a blood-curling shriek as he set a broken leg.

Trying to block out the screams, Leyn stuffed the chunk of bread into his mouth and added water, mixing them up by chewing vigorously.

"But you're eating it," Heike pointed out.

Leyn shook his head. He wanted to answer but realised just in time that he'd spray soaking bread and water at Heike if he did. He hastily covered his mouth with a hand.

That brought a wry smile to her face, one that lit up Leyn's heart. Some of the evening's terror faded as he recalled the way they had clutched onto each other on the reef. In sheer desperation then, but his memory now recalled the intimacy of their nearness. He'd never embraced a girl before.

He cupped a hand and worked the pulped bread out of his mouth. Heike pulled a face, and noted, "You're a strange boy, aren't you?"

Leyn shrugged. "It's to put on the cuts."

He reached for one of Heike's legs, eying a particularly nasty gash.

She scrambled to sit up, pulling her legs away. "*Hast du ein Wahn oder was?*[14] You're not putting your dirty hands on my leg."

Leyn blushed. He said, helplessly, "It's not what you think…the Doc…Niklas, he said to…"

There were more screams as Niklas set another broken bone.

Looking around, Leyn and Heike saw some of Niklas's other helpers chewing on bread and applying the paste to lacerated flesh.

Heike tentatively stretched out her legs again. "Alright then. But give me some bread and more water."

"It's not for…"

"Not for eating, I understand. For the others." Heike indicated the two women and children with a nod of her head. "They're cut up badly too. I can help."

"Thank you." Leyn broke off a bit of bread for her and held the water cask so she could take a mouthful.

As she chewed, he gingerly applied some of the bread paste to the long gash above her knee. Diligent as he tried to be, Leyn concluded guiltily that he was a sinner, unable to stop himself from taking in the curvature of Heike's legs

---

[14] *Hast du ein Wahn oder was?* German for 'are you delusional? Are you crazy?

and the sight of flesh revealed by scores of rips and cuts in her shift.

Leyn faintly registered that their troubles might not yet be over when he heard Jopie — back from the reef — make report to Rykert. The two had stepped aside from the larger group, within earshot of Leyn's corner.

"Half of them?" Leyn heard Rykert ask with anger in his voice.

"Aye, but there are more down there, they've been slipping away from the cave in twos and threes. It all went to hell when they found those casks of gin…"

"I'll go down there and show them what is what."

"Don't do that Boatswain. They say that without a ship or officers, they bain't bound to the Company."

"Mutiny? They dare mutiny?"

Leyn understood the disbelief in Rykert's voice. A chill crawled along his spine. Once mutiny was committed to there was no way back. The Company rules were clear in the verdict of death and detailed in the manner that punishment should be prolonged as long as possible, to inflict maximum suffering. The crew getting drunk on the reef had nothing to lose and everything to gain by persisting in their rebellion.

"Jopie, if any more of your men come up from the reef with salvage, keep them here."

"Aye-aye, Boatswain."

"Leyn."

Heike's voice got Leyn's attention. He blinked and looked at Heike, who was regarding him with a light frown but knowing smile.

"I think that's enough now." She indicated the last serious cut on a bared flank. The paste had been well and truly applied, but lost in his thoughts, Leyn's fingers had continued their soft strokes, this time along unscathed flesh.

Leyn snatched his hands away. "I'm sorry! I...I..."

Heike mocked him. "Ai, ai."

One of the lookouts came speeding into the cave, nearly colliding with Rykert.

"Boatswain! We saw movement outside!" The man panted between deep breaths.

Rykert asked eagerly, "Survivors? Natives?"

"Nay, animals of some kind. But...but... manlike, walking upright."

"By God's Gonads," Rykert cursed. He rushed out of the cave.

Leyn watched the boatswain leave, burning with curiosity.

"Go," Heike told him. She looked briefly at the others. "I'll finish the bread treatment. Go, see, and come back quick to tell us."

Leyn nodded. He needed no further encouragement to rush out of the cave, Jacob hot on his heels.

7. Osteoarchaeological Revelations

Arenes, Western Australia, 2016

Lette wasn't prepared for what she encountered in the Morgue. In her line of work human skeletal remains weren't uncommon. It certainly wasn't something that filled her with unease beyond the normal contemplation of life and death such a sight evoked. The sheer number of skeletons in the morgue tent, however, was astonishing. Rather than the grinning skulls and exposed rib cages, it was the multitude of them that was dreadful to behold.

"Quite a lot of them, aren't they?" One of the site crew approached them. It took Lette a moment to recognize Bruce, as he was now wearing glasses, a lab coat, and surgical gloves, as well as a far more serious expression on his face. The whole was somewhat countered by the fact that his lab coat hung open to reveal the same bared chest and miniscule shorts as before.

"I've worked on some of the graves found on Beacon Island," Bruce continued. "Which you may know better as Batavia's Graveyard. But other than the one mass grave there with five bodies, the ones I worked on were always in ones, or twos. Surprising, perhaps, considering that there must be over eighty bodies buried there. This here though..." he indicated the mass of tables behind him and shook his head.

"You've divided them into different groups," Lette noted.

"Indeed," Bruce answered. "The largest group here consists of some forty individuals. We found them in a burial field east of the larger cave. Each buried individually and with some care. That means each skeleton is reasonably intact. The next group over, ten individuals, were buried near that burial field, but all thrown into a mass grave, probably rather hastily. Then, at the far end of the tent, another eight or nine maybe even ten individuals. They were found about a mile east of the caves, in a couple of gullies out in the bush. Or rather, parts of them were found. So far we've been unable to assemble a complete body from those remnants."

"Those three at the far end of the large group seem smaller than the rest?" Lette noted.

"Aye," Bruce confirmed. "Two women and a youth. The latter with a gunshot entry point to the forehead and the back of his skull blown out."

"Women on a VOC ship?" Lette asked.

"In the early days it was fairly normal for soldiers sent out to the Indies to bring their families as passengers," Penning explained. "They curtailed that after *The Batavia* incident, as the VOC, in their wisdom, decided that appointing unbalanced men with severe mental health disorders as officers wasn't a source of trouble, but women on board clearly were."

Fieldman added, "After *The Batavia* it was just the high-ranking officials who were allowed – encouraged even – to bring over their families. Oh, and shipments of young orphans to be married off to VOC officials. Bruce, tell Lette about the injuries."

"Most curious," Bruce said. "Just about every individual here shows evidence of trauma."

This certainly wasn't Lette's area of expertise, so initially she thought of the kind of mental trauma that might well be inflicted by experiencing a shipwreck and mass death but then surmised that Bruce probably meant trauma of the bones. Tangible injuries that would leave forensic evidence even centuries after they had been inflicted.

"Injuries from the wreck?" Lette asked.

"We don't think that applies to most of them," Bruce said. "Bones or skulls splintered by musket balls. Bones or skulls that bear the marks of cuts by sharp blades, or else the impact of blunt objects. But then, look here, you see this femur? It was broken, but then set again, skillfully enough that I reckon it's the work of a ship's surgeon. That might be a shipwreck injury. But it never had time to heal. There's about half-a-dozen similar cases of fractures in this larger group. Somebody took the trouble to set the bones, but the healing process never took place."

"What does that mean?" Lette asked.

"Something terrible happened to the survivors of the wreck. All the evidence so far indicates that some sort of massacre took place, one likely conducted by human hand. But to confound us further, there is this…"

Bruce indicated that Lette should follow him to a corner of the tent that was partitioned off by screens. Moving one of the screens aside, Bruce revealed a larger table that bore the skeleton of an impossibly large creature, some three meters in length, with robust bones and a monstrous skull.

"Good grief!" Lette exclaimed. "What on earth is that?"

8. An Extraordinary Encounter

Arenes, The Southland, 1616

The boys scrambled up the mound until they reached Rykert and the handful of sailors on top. It had stopped raining, and the wind was at long last abating. The clouds were drifting apart. The day's light, only just improving after the storm induced gloam, was on the verge of dying.

To his right Leyn saw a score of sailors making up the scree, laden with casks, boxes, and sacks. They were staggering drunkenly. Govert Bastiaansz was with them, hollering louder than all the rest. Most of them had muskets slung over their shoulders.

Leyn realised that the weapons were from East Indiaman's armoury, packed in watertight crates.

Leyn looked the other way, inland. In front of him stretched an endless plain, covered by patches of shrub and low trees. There was some undulation, but only closer inspection revealed broad swells forming low ridges of a sort, as well as shallow gullies and zigzagging fissures cut into the bedrock. There were no signs of water or human habitation.

Nonetheless, five figures were cautiously approaching, seeming to move forward on three legs, the third leg protruding from their backside. They were incredibly tall, at least three meters, and possessed considerable muscular bulk, their chests and arms like those of a human prizefighter. Their upper bodies were bent forward a little, and although they carried no weapons or tools, those muscled arms looked like they could do some damage. They had flat, ape-like faces, with firm chins and eyes that were pointed forward, rather than at the sides like most animals Leyn knew of. Becoming aware of the humans in front of them, the creatures uttered soft inquisitive growls as their noses twitched when they sniffed at the air.

9. Bipedal Oddities

Arenes, Western Australia, 2016

"This skeleton belongs to a procoptodon goliah," Bruce said. "Short-faced giant kangaroos, if you will."

"Short-faced?" Lette asked.

"Unusually flat faces with snubbed snouts, with forward-pointing eyes and a developed chin," Bruce explained. "Like a primate. The smaller ones were on a par, size-wise, with the larger specimens of red kangaroos, but the goliah was easily twice as bulky, so it wouldn't have hopped like the roos we're familiar with. Instead, it was permanently bipedal, walking and standing upright, with the tail as a third leg to keep its balance. Add to that the typical human-like chest and arm musculature of a roo, and the goliah could be added to a cantina scene in Star Wars as a humanoid alien and George Lucas would be none the wiser."

"Don't be misled by that ferocious skull," Fieldman advised. "The upper and lower incisor teeth were to snip at leaves, the low-crowned molars indicate a herbivore, a browser, not a grazer, living off the leaves of shrubs and low trees."

"Like the vegetation on Arenes," Penning added.

"Still wouldn't pick a fight with it," Bruce said. "Indigenous people in New South Wales tell stories of large, long armed, and aggressive giant kangaroos. As you can see, this goliah has far longer and bulkier arms than a typical roo. I suspect it packs quite a punch."

"They've been found in South Australia, New South Wales, and Queensland," Fieldman said. "Common during the Pleistocene. Not our area of expertise, but we've done some homework after finding this. They were thought to have gone extinct about 18,000 years ago, but possibly even as close as 11,000 years ago."

*Becoming aware of the humans in front of them,
the creatures uttered soft inquisitive growls as their
noses twitched when they sniffed at the air.*

(Illustration by Julieann Williams)

10. Savages

Arenes, The Southland, 1616

The drunken mutineers reached the saddle that curved down between the larger mound Leyn was on and a slightly smaller mound to the south that also had a cave entrance on the seaward side.

Bastiaansz hollered, "Look! Savages!"

The other mutineers dropped their loads and whooped with derision.

The five creatures froze into perfect statues, staring intently at the shipwrecked Dutchmen on mound and saddle.

"Boatswain," Leyn called out, and pointed at the mutineers who were loading their muskets.

"Fools!" Rykert spat out. "You lot! Don't shoot at them."

His command was met with derisive laughter and vile insults. Rykert responded with a torrent of colourful expletives that did more to inform them about their dubious parentage than dissuade them from their murderous intentions.

Jacob tugged at Leyn's forearm. "Leyn! We're saved! Look, a ship."

Leyn looked at the ocean. His blood chilled as he registered the vague outline of a three-master, all of its red sails at full as if oblivious to the squalls that still pestered the wild waters. Once again, it was sailing directly into the wind.

More bad luck? We've had our share!

By the time Jacob drew the attention of the others the ship had vanished without a trace.

"It was there," Jacob insisted. "You saw her, didn't you, Leyn?"

Leyn didn't have a chance to answer. They all looked up at the sound of loud commands from the saddle.

"Ready!" Bastiaansz hollered. "Aim!"

Rykert tried to intervene, hollering. "Nay! Stop it you bloody fools!"

11. *Ay Baya!*

Arenes, Western Australia, 2016

"11,000 years," Lette mused. "So not necessarily related to our shipwreck survivors."

"That was our initial conclusion," Bruce said. "We're scientists, not peddlers of fairy tales. But then, how do we explain this?"

He pointed at one of the chunky leg bones and beckoned Lette to come closer. Intuitively glancing at the monstrous skull with irrational anxiety –

Of a long dead creature, Lette, she scolded herself. *It's not going to come back to life and hurt you.*

– she came closer and studied the bone. Her eyes found what Bruce wanted her to see, nestled tightly in the bone.

"There's another lodged deeply in the spine," he said.

"*AY BAYA!*"[15] Lette exclaimed. "A MUSKET BALL!"

---

[15] Expression of surprise in Sranantongo (Sranan), the informal language of Surinam

12. Might is Right

Arenes, The Southland, 1616

Bastiaansz grinned triumphantly, before roaring, "FIRE!"

A dozen muskets thundered. A cloud of gun smoke briefly enveloped the mutineers on the saddle before it was blown asunder by the wind.

Two of the creatures fell down, with agonised – almost human – screams of pain, bright red blood mixing with their brown fur. The other three scurried away at considerable speed, propelled by that third leg which Leyn now saw were actually long powerful tails.

The mutineers laughed and taunted the running creatures.

"Goddamn it," Rykert exclaimed with exasperation. "Those creatures might have led us to water. And now our presence will be known for miles around."

When the creatures were gone from view, the mutineers turned their mockery on the boatswain and his loyal crew. They were met with resigned silence and quickly grew bored. Gathering their haul and the two dead creatures, they made to the other smaller mound and dragged their spoils into the cave there.

Rykert gruffly told his men. "Enough of this madness. Back to work. Floris, maintain the watch."

13. Extant & Edible?

Arenes, Western Australia, 2016

"So the survivors encountered this goliah creature and shot it?" Lette asked. "Not quite extinct then, in the 17th century, unless this was the last one."

"It's not as farfetched as it might sound," Penning said. "The goliahs shared their habitat with red kangaroos and those are still around."

"Though we're keeping a lid on this for now," Fieldman added. "The press would have a field day if we reported shipwreck survivors encountering prehistoric giant kangaroos."

"It's believed that the procoptodon goliah became extinct because it was hunted by man," Bruce said. "They were by necessity bound to water sources, like humans, and easy to notice because of their great size."

"But as I mentioned to you," Fieldman added, "We've found no traces of human occupation of Arenes, until recent times when Maroons Cove was established. It's conceivable that the species survived here for much longer."

Penning pitched in. "It's been suggested that the goliah's closest living relative is the Banded Hare-wallaby. That species is still extant because it managed to survive on the islands of Bernier and Dorre, at the mouth of Shark Bay, not far from here. The lack of a human population there the likely cause of their survival."

Lette stared at the goliah bones. She, at least, had the advantage of being acquainted with kangaroos and wallabies which helped her envisage the appearance of a goliah. What would 17th century Dutchmen have made of a goliah, a creature entirely alien to their understanding of the world? She recalled how some of *The Batavia* survivors had encountered wallabies on what they had called High Island and Wiebbe Hayes's Island, now respectively known as East Wallabi Island and West Wallabi Island. They had dubbed the wallabies 'hopping cats' and had been delighted to discover that the animals were quite edible.

She wondered if the Arenes survivors had tried eating goliah. They probably had. If there was a running theme of Dutch maritime exploration it was that hungry Dutch sailors tried eating any creature they came across, from polar foxes on Nova Zembla, to the meat in native pemmican on the Hudson River, dodos on Mauritius, and 'hopping cats' on the Houtman Albrolhos.

She shook her head with disbelief at the notion that a Pleistocene species had managed to survive so long. *And unnoticed! What else might there be on the island?*

"If one species from the Pleistocene survived on Arenes," Lette ventured. "Could there have been others?"

Fieldman, Penning, and Bruce exchanged meaningful glances.

"It's possible," Bruce said. "In fact, it's likely. You'd best come and look at the last group of bones, the ones we found in the gullies to the east of the caves."

Lette followed him, noting the unease of the others as they approached the tables at the far end of the tent. She wondered what new surprise lay in store.

14. Suitably Contrite

Arenes, The Southland, 1616

Leyn and Jacob went back down to the cave.

They were stopped by an irate Niklas. "I told you to mind the patients in the corner."

"There were creatures," Leyn explained. "Animals, like giant apes."

"The mutineers were drunk and got muskets from the wreck and killed two of them," Jacob added.

Niklas sighed. "Then it's even worse than I thought. And you two are even bigger fools."

He sighed again when he saw their crestfallen expressions. "Those men are in the thrall of power, drunk and armed. Their blood is clearly already up. What do you think they'll do when they recall that there are female survivors?"

"Nay!" Leyn called out in horror. "They can't."

"That's the problem, lad. They can do anything they like, and we've got nothing to stop them. Now get to that corner and stay there. Do what you can to protect them. Keep them out of sight."

"Aye-aye, Doc."

The two ship's boys – looking suitably contrite – rejoined the corner's patients to report what they had seen.

"We heard the gunshots," Heike said.

Leyn nodded glumly. "There were some sort of local animals outside, the mutineers shot at them and killed two."

"So, these mutineers have muskets?" Heike asked, with concern in her voice.

Jacob sought a more positive perspective. "They also have gin. They'll drink themselves into a stupor."

Someone had managed to light a fire and before long small fires burned throughout the cave, fuelled by broken-up chests and spidery dead branches foraged in the immediate vicinity.

The foragers reported that the mutineer's cave was a source of drunken merriment, lending some weight to Jacob's prediction. There were also mouth-watering smells of roasting meat that drifted over from the other cave.

Leyn noticed that Rykert and the other old tars the boatswain relied on most, wore grave expressions and were fashioning lengths of wood into makeshift weapons.

The corner group sat huddled around their small fire, staring at the flames in silent thought.

Niklas came by to tell them to take some bread from the bread cask and share it between them. Leyn was so ravenous that he didn't even de-weevil his portion, chomping at the hard bread straight away, taking the juicy bits into his stride.

After their lean supper they started dozing off one by one. Leyn too was overcome by sheer exhaustion. Curling up on the sand as close to Heike as he dared, face toward the warmth of the fire, he fell asleep.

15. A Heartfelt One to One

Arenes, Western Australia, 2016

Lette and Karin Penning sat at one of the tables in the mess tent. Like everyone else, they had finished eating their dinner, which had consisted of sausages and chicken straight from the barbeque, roast potatoes, and coleslaw. Most of the others had gathered around some of the campfires that had been lit between the mess tent and the small township of tents where the crew slept. Somebody was strumming a guitar at one of the fires and others were singing along. Fittingly, it was an old sea-shanty.

> *There was a ship that sailed on the lowland sea*
> *It sailed by the name The Golden Vanity*
> *And we feared she would be taken*
> *By a Spanish galilee*
> *As we sailed upon the lowland, lowland, low*
> *As we sailed upon the lowland sea.*

"Some more gin?" Lette asked the professor, who was quick to agree that this was a splendid suggestion.

Lette had bought a bottle of Frisian *bessenjenever*[16] at one of the Schiphol Airport duty free shops before she had departed Amsterdam, and was pleased to have discovered that Penning was a fellow devotee of the stuff.

"*Bessenjenever* and *drop*," Penning toasted cheerfully.

---

[16] berry gin

"Are there other things you miss from the Netherlands?" Lette asked.

"Plenty," Penning answered. "But there are ample delights in Western Australia to make up for the loss. My work, for one. Don't you feel privileged to be here? Exploring this bit of ground? What was that English poem? A corner of a foreign field that is forever Holland."

"I think it mentions England, not Holland."

"Well then they got it quite wrong, didn't they? Silly people."

"I do feel privileged," Lette acknowledged. "To have seen all I have today, to have a puzzle to piece together. My mind is running riot trying to imagine what it must have been like back then. Stranded in an entirely strange environment, so far from home."

"Ah, the history disease," Penning nodded knowingly. "Can I ask you a personal question, Lette?"
"Of course."

"I have no doubt that we have similar experiences," Penning said. "Being women in a previously male-dominated field. Most of my colleagues accept me now, though there are always one or two who will give you that look of sympathetic pity, the 'oh the little woman has an opinion too' thing."

Lette grinned. "I know it well."

"I've always felt that I've had to work twice as hard to be acknowledged as a serious voice in our field. Which I don't mind all that much, because that has always motivated me to be the best of the best."

"You are!" Lette cried out, almost cringing at her own fan-girl tone but meaning every bit of it.

"Thank you. But I was wondering whether or not, uh, your ethnic origin…Surinam?"

"You want to know if it's even harder being a black woman in this field?"

"*Ja*, if you don't mind talking about it."

"Well, it is hard," Lette said. "There have been a few occasions that visitors to the museum I was due to meet assumed I was there to bring them coffee or tea. Or said things like 'could you mop the floor later, we're about to have an important meeting in here.'"

Penning snorted a laugh. "Oh, I'm sorry for laughing at that, it's just so ridiculous."

"Don't worry," Lette said with a smile. "I thought it was funny afterwards, especially when they were absolutely mortified when I explained who I was. But my primary reaction was anger. They clearly didn't expect me to have the capacity to fulfil a professional role at the museum."

"People are often pre-programmed with all of these pre-conceived notions."

"*Ja*, my fiancée experiences that too. Marvin's parents are from Surinam, like mine. He went to university, studied to become an economics teacher. But sometimes when he gets on the tram to go to work, in an eminently respectable profession and dressed formally, he'll note that people will clutch their bags tightly when they see a black man walking their way. Their assumption being that as a black man he'll probably try and snatch a purse, or something."

"Some more gin?" Lette asked the professor, who was quick to agree that this was a splendid suggestion.

(Illustration by Tom Brown)

Penning shook her head. "What a shite experience for him."

"It can be. We can usually laugh it off afterwards, but sometimes you just want to shake people by the shoulder and shout at them to make them understand that their behaviour is hurtful. Of course, if we did that, we'd be arrested for assault in a jiffy. Most cops would assume we're guilty as sin, again because of the skin colour."

"Unbelievable, in this day and age. Well, in the Netherlands anyway, the States is a whole different kettle of fish. It's still openly rife over there. They're even firing people just for being black, or for being a woman. People who have served the country for decades in the military, or NASA."[17]

"Or worse, fired simply for being a black woman." Lette nodded. "I had a teacher at school who had a little experiment. He'd ask the class to divide into two groups, one group for those who reckoned The Netherlands had risen above discrimination, and one group for those who believed discrimination was still very much a relevant social issue. He said that invariably most white students would join the group that believed discrimination to be a thing of the past and of no concern, whilst everyone else, those who actually experienced it on a daily basis, opted for the other group."

"Interesting. But then, let me confess to a preconception of my own. This field of ours. Fortunately, things have changed. We've begun to seriously address the

---

[17] A jump to 2025 where masculine fragility has indeed fallen this low.

wider implications of the whole VOC and WIC[18] endeavours, view colonialism anew. But originally, these studies were a celebration of the derring-do of our forefathers, getting on board of these small wooden ships and bravely sailing into the unknown, into danger. What has drawn you, with your background, to this field?"

"Can I reverse that question, professor? Why did you become interested in history?"

"An old cliché, I'm afraid. I believe that to understand our past helps us understand our present better, and potentially the future. And some personal interest as well. I have a forefather, Francois Penninck, from Veere in Zeeland. I know that he mustered as Second Mate on *De Loverendaal* and sailed to Batavia in 1738, returning in 1739 on *De Schellag*. By 1745 he was captain of *De Nieuwerkerk* and arrived in Batavia in that capacity after 256 days at sea. He died in 1747, while performing his duties in the East Indies. On the one hand, he contributed towards the colonial exploitation of the Indies, of which I cannot approve. On the other hand, I'm damned proud of him. I know that may sound funny, hypocritical even."

"Not at all," Lette said. "Regardless of the goal, braving the oceans was a courageous thing to do. But if you, as a white Dutch woman, set out in your career to understand your own past better, surely you can understand that a black woman might be driven by the same motivation? Why shouldn't I want to understand my past better? Willing or not, my very existence is a part of Dutch

---

[18] West Indies Company

colonial history. It's just that our ancestors were on these ships in different circumstances. Yours as commander on the quarterdeck. Mine, chained up below decks lying in their own excrement."

Penning laughed nervously. "*Ja*, of course."

"Don't get me wrong," Lette said. "I too admire the sense of adventure of your Francois Penninck. I don't believe that most of the sailors set out to deliberately construct an empire or oppress other people. When all is said and done, most were caught in the grind mill of poverty and trying to survive. The division isn't between black and white, the division is between rich and poor. And it has benefited the rich to turn one group of poor folk against another group of poor folk, by telling them they are better than the other group, and that they'd better be careful or else that other group will try to snatch their handbag in a busy tram or mop the floor when there's a meeting."

Penning chuckled. "You're a socialist then."

"Nay, not really. It's just the way I see the world. As you've said, perceptions are changing which is a good thing. But there is much more to be done, to educate people to not just blindly accept what they're told about the past. You see, in school, in history classes, we learned about the VOC and the WIC and the Dutch Empire. There's a nod toward the downsides of colonialism, but the 'we brought education, health, industry, transport' theme still runs strong. As if they did people a favour by stealing their land and labour. Then there's a reluctant acknowledgement that the Netherlands grew rich from the profits of slavery and that slavery 'might' not have been an entirely humane enterprise. But that's accompanied by the usual excuses. Everybody was doing it. The Arabs had slaves. Africans captured other Africans to sell as slaves. Asians had Asian slaves. The Spanish and Portuguese were way worse as slave masters so that justified the more 'humane' approach the Dutch and English claim to have had. Now that might ease the conscience of white pupils, but can you imagine what it's like, to be of Surinam or Indonesian origin and to be spoon-fed this stuff? Because an inherent part of this is the so-called White Man's Burden, the notion that we're allowed to sit at your table now because we've assimilated like good little girls and boys. That we've been saved from supposed primitive savagery, so to speak. But that back then we were just barbarians, with no culture to speak of, no concept of human morality that sufficed to be seen on an equal basis."

"I've never really thought about it that deeply from this perspective," Penning admitted.

"Like we established, people are pre-conditioned. Surinamese people too. I attended the *Openbare Schoolgemeenschap Bijlmer*, the OSB in the Bijlmer[19], which the Dutch, with their lack of subtlety, call a 'black school' because that was the dominant skin colour. Even there we were taught this version of history. We were taught that the Dutch discovered Australia, for example, before the English did. But what about the Indigenous people of Australia? Who might well be surprised to be told that a

---

[19] The Bijlmer is an outskirt of Amsterdam where a majority of the inhabitants are of Surinamese origin.

land they had lived in for millennia had suddenly been 'discovered'? Or else, didn't count as relevant or important until the Europeans came? Same for Indonesia. In Dutch schools, Indonesia came into existence when the Dutch arrived. Never mind the thousands of years of a rich cultural heritage that had developed on those islands before the Dutch made an entry. I'm sorry professor, I seem to be lecturing you!"

"Please, continue. You have my ear."

Lette nodded appreciatively but paused to take a few deep breaths. She knew that once she got going on this subject she could carry on for hours. It made a lot of people uncomfortable, but Professor Penning seemed genuinely fascinated. "At the OSB, being a 'black school', expectations were low. Not necessarily from our own teachers, but from the educational system. That teacher I spoke about, he taught English. He explained that when he'd taught English at white schools he'd be tied by a predetermined curriculum with detailed instructions as to what items of grammar to teach, learning objectives, assessments, the SMART model, success criteria...all that malarkey. At the OSB he received a very brief instruction. 'Acquaint them with aspects of Anglo-American culture and a bit of language.' That was all. And could he please fill two years with that until our exams."

"That's disgraceful," Penning commented.

Lette shook her head. "It was a blessing. He said he'd always dreamed of being able to do what that teacher in that movie *Dead Poet Society* did, ripping up the curriculum and focusing on the important stuff. He saw it as a challenge and in devising his lessons he took the composition of his classes into account. He made education *relevant*. He taught us about the American Civil Rights struggle, Rosa Parker, Ruby Bridges, Martin Luther King, Malcolm X, and before that Harriet Tubman. He made us read *Roll of Thunder, Hear My Cry* by Mildred Taylor, watch *To Kill a Mockingbird* and *Mississippi Burning*. We analysed Nina Simone songs. We introduced him to rap, and he promptly incorporated that into his lessons. Then he covered the anti-apartheid struggle in South Africa, and we got to know about Mandela, Tambo, Tutu, Sisulu, Biko, and Kogbara. Our English improved with leaps and bounds, though he never really spent much time going on about grammar. He figured we'd learn through working with English language materials. And at the end of those two years, all his classes performed above the national average in the exams. Kids from a 'black school' showing what they were worth! But most importantly, I think, is what one of my classmates told him. 'You are the first to teach me that black people can be heroes.' And in my case, the first to teach me that black women can be heroes. Can you imagine that professor? I was seventeen years old, and nobody had ever bothered to tell me that. All the role models I had been presented with were white, white men at that, and I had just about concluded that I could never aspire to that because we were, well, we were 'just' black and therefore not good enough."

The singers around the campfire had advanced to bawdy songs and were giving a cheerful rendition of *A Lusty Young Smith*.

With a jingle-bang, jingle-bang, jingle-bang, jingle,
With a jingle-bang, jingle-bang, jingle, hi ho!

"Powerful stuff," Penning said. "I should have liked to have met this teacher of yours."

"He retired from teaching. His style of teaching, encouraging us to think outside of the box, clashed with the Dutch educational system."

"And you feel an obligation to pick up the torch?"

"*Ja*, I do. I applied to do my bachelor's degree at Uni, because, why not? I finally believed I was good enough. And a master's after that. And then infiltrated a former bastion of colonialism. As I said, it's my history too and I feel that I have a relevant voice, my experience counts too. I don't want to just be a passive subject of that history, but play a more active role, be one of the constructive narrators.

"And it's not just me, or black folk. This is a global development. The First Nations in Canada and the States are demanding to be heard. There are Indonesian voices in the Netherlands who believe that their version of our common history deserves equal merit. Here in Australia, I think the Indigenous people have had enough of being condemned to a lower tier. The Maori in New Zealand, well, they can serve as an example to us all, really."

"Leading to whole tribes of white men hollering that they are being oppressed," Penning grinned.

"They don't get it. Of course their voice counts. But not just theirs, ours too. Our common history isn't their exclusive domain. The whole planet, for that matter, is one to be shared, not to be the property of a single demographic."

"Have you considered doing a PhD?"

"A PhD? Me?" Lette shook her head. "I'm just..."

"Black?" Penning asked with a mischievous smile.

Lette laughed. "Touché."

"Lette, I would be honoured, truly honoured, to be your mentor and supervisor. That way I can help you in your mission. It's been a long time since I've encountered someone as driven as you and we definitely need to move away from the purely Eurocentric perspective. I reckon you have the potential to have an exemplary career ahead of you. You could be that missing role model for other girls in the Bijlmer. Is that not something to work toward?"

"Really?" Lette asked. Even though the offer had been made, it was difficult to conceive of the notion of working closely with this living legend.

"Think on it, and we'll talk about the practicalities some more later," Penning said. "Though do be aware that I will nag you endlessly and I usually get my way."

"Thank you, Professor."

It had got dark while they had been talking. As the moon rose over the edge of the Arenes plateau, all hell broke loose in the bush, a cacophony of chaos.

Lette looked in that direction with some consternation.

"Ah," Penning said. "Nobody warned you?"

"Warned me about what?"

16. Moonlit Promises

Arenes, The Southland, 1616

"Leyn. Leyn."

Leyn reluctantly woke when Heike repeated his name, speaking softly.

Leyn struggled to emerge from his sleep. "Wazzizit?"

"Listen!"

"Huh?"

"Can you hear those sounds?"

Leyn registered a faint hullabaloo outside. "What the hell?"

"Come. Let's find out what it is."

Leyn looked around. The dying fires within the cave cast a soft glow on the walls, pillars, and sleeping forms on the sand. Outside there was nothing but darkness. "I'm supposed to stay here."

"All right then." Heike shrugged. "I'll go out alone."

She got to her feet and walked towards the cave's gaping mouth. For a fleeting moment the light fall clearly outlined her body beneath her shift, causing Leyn to become dizzy with an overwhelming desire he had never experienced before and a strong protective urge. That last, he knew, was ridiculous, as it seemed that the strong-willed Heike had been looking after him rather than the other way around. The strange yearning, however, was oh so real.

"Wait," Leyn called out softly and scrambled up to follow her. He was sure Niklas wouldn't want Heike to go out on her own.

Once his eyes had adjusted it was surprisingly light outside. The sky was clearing rapidly and had unveiled a waxing moon bright enough to cast a ghostly pale glow on the landscape. The earlier dry and dusty taste of the air had been replaced by a fresher, sweet fragrance.

He could see the dying glow of a fire emanating from the mutineer's cave, but it appeared bereft of the earlier intoxicated tide of uproar, although it was hard to tell with the native din that had replaced it. What had sounded like a continuous hum inside the cave seemed overpowering outside. A hubbub of different sounds that combined to make a disharmonious concerto of the night.

Leyn and Heike walked around the mound, rather than climbing it and disturbing the sentries on top, until they had a view of the endless plain shimmering in the moonlight. A multitude of stars appeared in the expanding gaps between the remnants of the clouds.

The clamour was hard to pinpoint, it seemed to be coming from everywhere in bits and pieces, other than the shrill and penetrating drone from cicadas that was continuous and all encompassing.

"It's as if the very land is singing," Heike said in wonder. "The trees and bushes, the rocks."

"And animals," Leyn added, as he identified animalistic gurgles, yelps, hoots, and cries.

Heike said, "Niklas said that he reckoned we're on the Isle of Arenes. It's so beautiful here!"

"Beautiful?" Leyn asked doubtfully. Although the land's song with its eerie reverberations and haunting cries was mesmerising somehow, the place still looked barren and desolate to him.

"You would think so too," Heike declared firmly. "If you'd been locked up in the orlop for months on end, listening to men snore, grunt, belch and fart. The stench was incredible. It's so good to breathe clean air. Today was terrible. Our lot was vomiting all day. Your lot threw shit down on us. *So ein Misthaufen!*[20] Literally! A nightmare. I thought it would never end."

She shuddered.

"I didn't," Leyn said quickly. "Throw shit. I refused to. I went…I used the head."

Heike bobbed a sarcastic curtsy at him. "Thank you, Leyn, for not shitting on me."

Leyn nodded happily, amazed that he was having an actual conversation with a girl and not making a total mess of it. Not just any girl either, but beautiful and beguiling Heike, delivered from the grasp of the furious ocean.

The hum, buzz, and cries continued to wash over them, hauntingly hypnotic, though now adding menacing growls and snorts.

"Why did you come?" Leyn asked. "The trip is hard as nails, everybody knows that."

"We lost our parents to a plague. This was the only job that Bertram could get. He said that if we survived the fevers we could have a proper future in the Indies."

---

[20] *So ein Misthaufen,* German for 'what a heap of manure' used as in 'what a pile of crap'.

Not just any girl either, but beautiful and beguiling Heike, delivered from the grasp of the furious ocean.
(Illustration by Tom Brown)

Heike was moving her head around as she tuned into the resonance of the land's song. Her expression of deep wonder formed a contrast to the pain in her voice. "I could have chosen to stay. But in an orphanage with strangers. That was too horrible to even think about. What about your family?"

Leyn shrugged. "I've got none. The orphanage thing."

"Oh!" Heike sounded embarrassed.

"Nay, you were right. It really is too horrible to even think about. I was pleased when they sold me to the Company. I like being a ship's boy most of the time. I haven't been homesick at all."

"I have," Heike said, crestfallen. "I miss Saxony. Even Holland and Zeeland." After a moment's pause, she added. "And now I have no one left at all."

Leyn's head spun as if the ocean was tumbling him about in a turbulent embrace. Had there been soft suggestion in her tone when she said that last?

"You have me," he pronounced bravely, investing the words with the solemnity of a promise, but unable to keep out an undertone of worry that she might think him silly.

The moon's beams highlighted Heike's response – a warm smile. "I know."

Leyn's eyes widened. The land's song changed into a potent, pulsing throb that quickened the increasing frequency of otherworldly hoots, harrowing ululations, and bestial snarls. He leaned forward, hoping for a kiss.

"But now is not the best time…" Heike's voice trailed off. "What was that!"

"What?"

Leyn's universe had momentarily consisted only of Heike, with no room for anything else. The desolation of Arenes reappeared in his awareness. Heike pointed at a gully, a few hundred meters away. Leyn could see nothing but a patchwork of dark shadows contrasted by the pale shimmer of moonlit ground and brush. All he sensed, regretfully, was the poignant waning of a magical moment of togetherness that seemed to be slipping out of his grasp.

All still. Nay, wait. There!

"There!" Heike pointed again.

"Aye, I see."

Something was moving along the bottom of the gully. Bounding forward on all fours. Once he had seen the first, Leyn made out more such crouched figures moving forward in silent determination.

The land's song turned into a menacing cacophony of barks, screams and hoots, lent depth by the continuous throbbing drone of cicadas.

17. Birds of a Feather

Arenes, Western Australia, 2016

Lette and Penning walked to the edge of the camp to overlook the plains that had suddenly become so noisy. Lette could place the unceasing chirping of the cicadas, though was somewhat surprised by how deafening it was out here. But there were far more noises that seemed unworldly somehow, or downright disturbing.

"The lack of human habitation on the plateau has made Arenes somewhat of a bird's paradise," Penning explained. "There are feathered friends from all over the country here, even if they're usually just bound to the east or south coast. You hear that low frequency grumble?"

"Like a lion growling," Lette agreed.

"A cassowary."

Something seemed to cackle like a maniac, answered by similar sounds of deranged laughter.

"Someone forgot to lock the lunatic asylum?" Lette guessed.

Penning chuckled. "Kookaburras. And that low ghostly wailing you hear is a tawny frogmouth. You'll get used to it, but the first night I was out here it freaked me out big time, I don't mind admitting."

Something uttered a shrill scream that caused Lette to flinch. It sounded like a woman crying out in terrified distress.

"That would be a bush stone curlew," Penning said. "And…wait for it."

The shrieks of anguish were suddenly echoed across the plain.

"Lyrebirds," Penning explained. "They have an astonishing ability to mimic sounds. I've heard one imitate a chainsaw once, believe it or not."

"They wouldn't even believe this back home," Lette said.

"Not quite like the Vondel Park in the Dam, is it?"

"More like the soundtrack of a Hieronymus Bosch painting."

Penning laughed. "Very eloquently put. I think I'll steal that."

"The soundtrack of a Hieronymus Bosch painting."

(Illustration by Julieann Williams)

18. At the Mercy of Brutes

Arenes, The Southland, 1616

Leyn and Heike were distracted by commotion at the cave. Angry voices, some invested with intoxicated audacity. They rushed back until they were nearly in sight of the cave's broad mouth and then hugged the mound's flank for cover.

The light that emanated from the cave cast a red glow on two groups of men, lined up and facing each other. The smaller line was formed by Boatswain Rykert and his most loyal men: Floris, Jopie, Nelisz, Willem, and a few others. Opposite them were a score of mutineers, many of them armed with muskets, the triumph of power clear on their faces.

"Can't you get it through your thick skulls?" Rykert growled at them. "We're stranded God knows where! We need to work together to survive."

"We need to eat to survive," Bastiaansz countered. "You're wasting bread on wounded folk likely to die anyway."

"Dutch folk," Jopie called out in disbelief and outrage. "Shipmates. *Our* folk."

"Shut up," Bastiaansz commanded. "We want all you salvaged from the wreck. Bread, water, and anything else."

Rykert shook his head in disgusted denial.

Bastiaansz added with a leer. "And we want the women."

The other mutineers cheered and voiced their agreement. "Hand over the women. Give us the women."

Leyn felt Heike shudder. He placed a hand on her shoulder, for comfort and reassurance, but she pulled away from him.

"Leyn, we have to run."

He shook his head, placing his confidence in Rykert.

"Well, you're not getting all you want," Rykert boomed. "Let's talk about this. We can spare some water and bread."

Bastiaansz's answer was short. "Shoot them. Fire!"

The armed mutineers triggered their muskets. The weapons spat out blinding flashes and deadly lead at near point-blank range. Cries of pain sounded as Rykert and some of his men fell to the ground.

Loud yells of shocked fear sounded from within the cave. The ominous droning, shrieking, hooting, and growling of the land's song was mixed with outraged yelps, as if offence was taken at the intrusion of man-made thunder.

Leyn made to run toward the cowardly murderers in a furious rage, but Heike restrained him, repeating, "We have to run."

"Kill the rest of 'em!" Bastiaansz commanded, and the mutineers followed his order with enthusiasm, drawing cutlasses and quickly overwhelming Rykert's remaining men.

"We can't just..." Leyn looked on helplessly.

"You want to live, or die?"

"The cave is ours!" Bastiaansz trumpeted.

The mutineers cheered and most of them ran into the cave, waving their bloodied cutlasses. Their entry was quickly followed by panicked shouts and screams of pain.

Horrified as he was by the sounds of carnage, Leyn let Heike grab his hand and pull him away.

"There's no fighting this madness," Heike hissed.

They had barely progressed fifty meters along the ridge, crashing haphazardly through the brush, when somebody called out Leyn's name.

Leyn turned to see Jacob running after them, followed by the two children. The three were pursued by Govert Bastiaansz and one of the other mutineers, both carrying a musket.

"Wait for us!" Jacob yelled.

"Help us! Save us!" the little boy begged.

Then he screamed because Bastiaansz had come close enough to grab the lad's hair and yank him to a painful stop.

"Nay! You bastard!" Jacob cried out, turning and making to dash toward the terrified child.

A loud bang sounded as the other mutineer triggered his musket. The shot hit Jacob's face and blew out the back of his skull, sending a spray of wet droplets at Leyn and Heike – who stood, frozen.

Bastiaansz laughed loudly at the horror on their faces, shouldered his musket, and then twisted the howling boy around to punch him hard in the face. The boy dropped like a sack of flour. When the girl shrieked her terror at this sight, Bastiaansz punched her hard enough to knock her out too.

Bastiaansz called out cheerfully. "Why, it's my lucky day. It's the little scrotum-sack." He took in Heike with ravenous appetite in his eyes. "I'll be the first to fuck your little bitch, Jonas. And I'll let you watch me do it."

"Run!" Leyn and Heike called out simultaneously, even as they turned. They pounded through the brush, desperate to get away from the brutes who had just murdered Jacob in cold blood.

The land's song reached a frantic pitch and tempo and added what sounded like manic insane laughter to its repertoire. Heike stumbled and fell, rolling over the ground until she was stopped by the resistance of a low bush.

The two mutineers had been swift to pursue and were hot on their heels.

Bastiaansz hollered, "Ha! Got you now."

Leyn stopped to help Heike scramble up. He knew he likely doomed himself by the action, but didn't hesitate.

Bastiaansz caught up with them before Heike had fully risen to her feet. He gave them an almighty shove with the stock of his musket, knocking them both to the ground.

Leyn fell flat on his back. He couldn't breathe. The musket's stock had knocked the air out of him. His vision was blurred. Heike clutched him, calling out his name. He was vaguely aware of Bastiaansz towering over them, flanked by the other mutineer.

Leyn gasped at the air, choking, struggling in Heike's hold. *I'm going to die. Here and now.*

Bastiaansz – still no more than a bulky smudge – was preaching something incomprehensible, his tone one of boastful gloating. He knew he had Leyn and Heike at his

Bastiaansz hollered, "Ha! Got you now."

(Illustration by Tom Brown)

mercy and hoped to goad them into resistance – to be swiftly punished – or into submission, begging at his feet. Either option wouldn't alter the outcome of the confrontation, and both would be equally entertaining for Bastiaansz.

"*Schleich dich! Verpiss dich!*[21]" Heike hissed and spat her fury at Bastiaansz in a torrent of angry German words. He responded with vile promises as to his intentions with her.

Leyn managed to ingest some air, cough it out, and then draw in a deeper and sweeter breath. He marvelled that he lived as he drank in the cool night air.

Loud deep grunts and growls briefly overpowered all the other nighttime sounds, causing both Bastiaansz and Heike to fall silent simultaneously.

"There's something out there," the other mutineer told Bastiaansz nervously.

---

[21] *Schleich dich, verpiss dich* – German for respectively 'get lost' and 'piss off'

19. An Exercise in Insanity

Arenes, Western Australia, 2016

Lette was woken at the crack of dawn by Fieldman urgently calling out her name outside of the tent she had been assigned.

She grumbled a protest, but Fieldman was having none of it. "We've got to seize the rare opportunities we get, Lette," he insisted. "To get a closer look at that wreck. Come to the mess tent, there's hot coffee. We're heading down in twenty minutes."

That was sufficient to get Lette crawling out of her sleeping bag, hastily dressing, and then stumbling to the mess tent where Bruce pressed a mug of steaming coffee into her hands.

There were over a dozen others there, including Bruce, Fieldman, and Penning.

"It's an extreme low tide this morning," Penning explained. "Meaning we might be able to get visuals on some of the prominent features of the wreck."

"Not to mention consider an exercise in insanity," Bruce said mysteriously.

"Good," Lette sipped her coffee. "I like exercises in insanity."

"That will be most handy," Penning predicted.

They made their way to the shoreline platform. Lette was glad that she was able to descend the scree slope unencumbered, unlike some of the other younger members of the team who carried various bundles and boxes of equipment. The scree was as treacherous as Martin Fieldman had said it would be when she first arrived.

The first advantage that Lette noticed about the extreme low tide was that there were no waves bashing against the shoreline platform's edges to shower them in spray. The second was that the sea was becalmed enough for them to be able to discern one of the anchors where the bow had buried itself onto the reef, as well as the distinct shapes of the cannons on the seabed.

Some of the crew had taken out previously sketched *in situ* maps of the wreck and were comparing these to the visual overview the low tide offered, scribbling notes. Most, however, had gathered around one of the larger blowholes, peering down it with a combination of tension and rising excitement.

Beginning to understand what Bruce had meant by an exercise in insanity, Lette quickly joined them.

Bruce was on his knees, shining a powerful torch down the blowhole. It formed an uneven narrow chute, lined with jagged coral. At the bottom – some six meters down – was wet, but sandy ground.

"As I thought," Bruce said happily. "I reckon it's feasible."

Fieldman was doubtful. "It'll be risky."

"No fun if it isn't risky," Bruce said. "But I reckon I can get down there to have a look. Please Martin, it'll be a rare opportunity to get a closer look at the undercut. Logically speaking, there will be debris from the wreck that's been swept beneath the platform."

Fieldman nodded. "That's a very strong possibility. But this isn't a game for old folk like me, Bruce."

"Nor me," Penning said. She glanced at Lette.

Recalling what they had discussed the night before about taking her studies further, Lette recognised the opportunity to possibly make an actual *in situ* discovery. "I'll go."

"And me," one of the younger men said.

"Very well," Fieldman said. "But I want you all to don a wet suit. That will offer at least some protection against that coral. And any sign of trouble or danger down there, you come straight back up, do you understand?"

The three volunteers nodded and then proceeded to get into the wet suits that had been brought down. Others constructed a sturdy frame from metal tubes that was placed over the blowhole. When the three volunteers were in their wet suits they were helped into safety harnesses. Lette was relieved that she wasn't expected to clamber down a rope but would be lowered down the blowhole instead.

"One at a time," Bruce said. "I'll go first, as it was my idea, and I should be the first to experience any…discomfort there might be."

He donned a climbing helmet with an inbuilt torch on top and secured the strap beneath his chin. Safety lines were clasped to his harness. He was then helped to position himself in the frame over the blowhole and lowered down ever so slowly, to avoid rapid friction with the sharp coral.

"Made it," he called up. "Ground beneath my feet is solid enough."

"Test each step though," Penning called down. "Take it real slow. And wait until the rest get down."

Lette was next to don her helmet. It felt awkward to position herself over the hole lumbered in the wet suit with the harness, but the actual descent was no bother, other than the claustrophobic sense of being in a very narrow space with coral rock surrounding her on all sides. She was relieved when she sensed more space around her and delighted when her feet struck the ground. Bruce helped her unclasp the lines from her harness and then signalled that the lines could be hauled up again for the last volunteer.

Lette looked around her as the third person was lowered down. They were in a low dome of sorts. She could stand upright in the centre of it, but the ceiling sloped down to the ground – a flat bed of wet sand – all around them, except towards the ocean, where a narrow and low passage led out of the chamber. It stood to reason that this passage was how the water reached the blowhole, but would it remain wide enough to allow them to squeeze through?

When they were ready to find out Bruce led the way. The going was extremely slow, with Bruce testing the ability of the sand to hold his weight step by step, taking his time to ensure that the ground underfoot was safe. Their snail-like speed was frustrating, but Lette understood the danger of one of them sinking into the sand down here. The corridor required them to crouch down but was wide enough for them to pass through. After taking two sharp turns, it widened again, with the ceiling rising until they came to a wide chamber, with daylight peeping inside from a low but wide entrance on the far side.

Bruce was the first to get a look at the chamber and uttered an astonished "Fucking hell!" before adding, "Rock underfoot, we're safe here."

He shuffled aside to let Lette enter the chamber. She gasped, then remembered to step aside to let the third volunteer in on their discovery.

Their heads swept from side to side to allow their helmet torches to illuminate the chamber floor. The first meter or so was just a rocky ledge that allowed them safe footing. The rest of the chamber, at least four meters wide and eight meters long, was carpeted with silver coins, from dripping wall to dripping wall. Although dulled somewhat, and apparently fused by lime, it seemed that the coins had barely been touched by erosive processes, nor were they encrusted other than a faint green tint on some of them and the lime that cemented stacks of them together. As a result, the coins lit up whenever the torchlight rested upon them, shining brightly. To add to the piratical flavour of the scene, three bodies had been washed into the chamber as well. Tucked into horizontal niches along the walls, their skeletal remains were mostly whole, grinning skulls with dark gaping eye sockets and all.

"Talk about a jackpot," Bruce said, choking up a bit.

Lette could only nod, still speechless. This was the sort of rare find most could only dream about.

They hurried back to the blowhole chamber, assuming now that they had tested the sandy footing sufficiently to know it was safe.

Bruce shouted up their news, "A carpet of silver!"

This was met by loud cheers from those over ground. There was a consultation of sorts, shouted up and down the blowhole, even as some equipment began to be lowered down, including photo and video cameras and tripods.

Time became a headache now. Those beneath the platform would have to bring themselves and their equipment back up before the tide rolled back in to flood the silver cave and blowhole chamber. If they had been mere treasure seekers it would have been a matter of scooping up as many coins as possible while they could, but as professionals they couldn't simply start disturbing the site willy-nilly.

The plan was to mark out about a square meter, and document that square meter carefully before the material within the marked area could be removed for further study. The rest of the silver carpet would have to be surrendered back to the ocean until another opportunity arose.

When the surface of the marked area had been documented, a first dozen coins or so were carefully placed in a plastic container filled with salt water to be raised to the surface and then brought to the special conservation tent in Camp Whoop Whoop. Lette accompanied this first retrieved material back up to the over ground, in order to escort these first coins back to camp. She was patted on the back by the ecstatic over ground crew whose sheer delight at the day's success could barely be contained, although that box was treated reverently and with extreme care. Lette was helped out of her harness and wet suit, even as two other volunteers donned theirs, to reinforce the small team beneath the reef.

The climb up the scree slope was excruciatingly slow, with two of the crew ever so carefully carrying the box up. The last thing they wanted was to drop the box and spill the coins across the scree.

A technician at the conservation tent took the box gingerly and then expressed her delight at the well-preserved state of the coins.

"Electrolysis," she told Lette. "The full process might take a week, or longer, but the moment we can discern a minting date, you'll be the first to know."

"How long?" Lette asked impatiently. She knew that rushing things was ever a no-no, but a concrete date would help her narrow down her search perimeters to such an extent that finding answers would become much easier. Climbing down blowholes was exciting to be sure, finding that silver carpet would no doubt remain a highlight of her career, but that wasn't why she'd flown Down Under. It was her archival expertise that would allow her to make a valuable contribution.

"Sorry, I don't want to make any promises I might not be able to keep," the technician answered.

Lette accepted this and promised to wait patiently. Easier said than done, of course. Not one for sitting around twiddling her thumbs, she wandered into the Landlubber's HQ tent to gaze again upon the finds so far. It had seemed like a veritable treasure the day before, but now, with her mind's eye returning to the silver carpet again and again, she had to remind herself that a broken clay pipe had as much of a story to tell as a silver coin.

She mused upon Karin Penning's offer. Accepting it would mean spending a lot of time in Western Australia. The National Maritime Museum in Amsterdam, Lette reckoned, would offer support and allow for a leave of absence. Marvin wouldn't like her being so far away for a prolonged period, but he was proud of her achievements and always encouraged her to take up opportunities to further her career. As for her parents, why they were proud as peacocks and always offered their full support in any endeavour Lette undertook, because that's what parents were for. None of the potential obstacles, Lette reasoned, were insurmountable and the prospect of working with Penning and living in Western Australia for a stretch appealed to her a great deal.

Next, Lette drifted into the Morgue. It was empty, well, at least empty of living beings, for all the skulls seemed to stare at Lette accusingly as if they were aware that she had uncovered one of the wreck's well-guarded secrets.

"I will try to name you," she promised vaguely, immediately feeling foolish for talking to skeletons.

Drawn by the tables at the far end of the tent, Lette made her way over, recalling what Bruce, Fieldman, and Penning had revealed about the remnants there the day before.

As Bruce had said, there were no whole skeletons retrieved from the gullies where they had been found. Currently the bones and bone fragments were grouped together according to Bruce's best estimates as to which ones belonged together – until DNA tests could be done –, but there was a large *in situ* map that revealed in what a disordered jumble the bones had been found.

"Literally torn apart," Bruce had said. "That might have been the work of scavengers, but there are indications of something else at work."

He had shown her pits, scores, punctures and furrowing marks on the bones. Almost half the bones bore these scars.

"A predator's teeth marks," Bruce had said. "A large predator."

Lette had frowned. She had vague notions that Australia was filled with all sorts of deadly flora and fauna but had to admit that most of her knowledge stemmed from internet memes designed to poke fun at this. Yet other than crocodiles and sharks, unlikely to inhabit dry gullies in the bush, no obvious candidates had come to mind.

"Dingos?" She had ventured. "Some sort of Tasmanian Devil?"

"Too small," Bruce had answered. "We're looking at an animal about the size of an African lioness."

"Lions? In Australia?"

"It made no sense to us either. Until we took the Pleistocene context into consideration. If the procoptodon goliah had remained extant on Arenes, might there not be other survivors from the Pleistocene here, far-fetched as that might seem?"

"And there was a candidate," Fieldman had said. "The thylacoleo carnifex."

"Marsupial lions," Penning had added.

"We need to be careful, of course," Bruce had continued. "I am by no means specialised in prehistoric fossils and the danger in a case like this is that you see what you want to see. But look at these marks..." He pointed them out, "Those were made by blade-like teeth that were at least three centimetres long. And see these acutely angled 'V' shaped edges? Those are tell-tale signs of the thylacoleo carnifex." He had turned the bone over. "The same mark, so opposing marks, suggesting the bone was seized between lower and upper jaw."

"No chance of it being a stray tiger? They did have them in the Indies, far away perhaps, but not impossibly so."

Bruce had replaced the bone and dug some images from a file. He had placed three pictures next to each other; one photograph of a tiger with an open jaw, the second a photograph of a lion with an open jaw. The third had been an artist's depiction of a creature that looked somewhat like a catlike bear, open-mouthed like the others, but with the bottom of its chin leaning on forepaws with claws that looked out of place. Puzzling over the paws, Lette had realised that not only did the marsupial lion have opposable thumbs, but that those thumbs were absurdly large with long, wicked looking, curved claws.

"The dentition of a marsupial lion is unlike that of any other mammalian carnivore." Bruce had said. "Compare. The tiger and lion have greatly enlarged upper and lower canines, as do other felines, as well as dogs, wolves, and bears. For them, the canines are the primary killing tool. Our marsupial friend now, has no canines in the lower jaw and only tiny canines in the upper jaw. But look at its incisor teeth."

"They are huge," Lette had marvelled.

"Protruding forward, ideal for stabbing with. Then look at the carnassial teeth, the side cheek teeth as it were. They are oversized in comparison to the tiger or lion. They are in essence enormously long shearing blades, for slicing. Other differences are that, like other marsupials, the thylacoleo carnifex was able to use its tail, shorter but far bulkier and muscular than a big cat's, to help it balance on its hind legs, leaving its forelegs free to catch or handle prey. Their forelegs are incredibly powerful and have a unique elbow joint that would allow for rotational capacity and far more foreleg and paw manipulation than we see with lions or tigers. It also has the most powerful bite of any mammalian predator, extant or extinct."

"The theory is," Fieldman had said. "That these marsupial lions were highly specialised meat-eaters. They weren't great runners, like lions. Indigenous depictions indicate striped fur, the camouflage required by a predator like a tiger, that hunts not on open plains, but ambushes in densely vegetated areas."

"Low trees and shrubs, like Arenes," Bruce had added.

"Using those thumb claws, then?" Lette had asked.

"Indeed," Bruce had agreed. "While the other big cats catch their prey and hold in it place with their claws whilst using their razor-sharp canines for the kill, the thylacoleo probably did the opposite, stabbing with those incisors and using its jaws to hold an animal still, presumably around the throat area, and then using its stabbing claws to disembowel the prey as the primary means of killing it."

Lette had shuddered. "And the teeth marks on the bones, unique to this marsupial lion, suggests that the shipwreck survivors encountered one of these creatures, extant still, on Arenes?"

"Close, but not entirely," Bruce had answered. "Fossil finds suggest that the thylacoleo took on prey larger than itself, such as goliahs, or much larger than itself, like the diprotodon. That is far easier if the predator isn't a solitary hunter. Moreover, fossil finds in caves suggest that the thylacoleos were social animals."

"In other words," Fieldman had concluded. "These marsupial lions lived and hunted in packs. The survivors are likely to have encountered more than one."

Recalling all this, Lette shivered. Those shipwreck survivors, she reckoned, had faced far more dangers than they might have bargained for.

"Miss Sabajo?"

Tearing her mind away from the unnerving image of a thylacoleo carnifex, Lette turned to see that the conservation tent technician she had spoken to earlier had entered the Morgue.

"Miss Sabajo," the woman beamed. "We have a date for you."

It also has the most powerful bite of any mammalian predator, extant or extinct.

(Illustration by Tom Brown)

20. *Was Zum Teufel?*

Arenes, The Southland, 1616

Heike came into focus, and Leyn smiled at her as if they were alone and nothing else mattered. "You were right Heike, it's beautiful here. So are you."

"Hush," she whispered, looking around them warily. Funnily enough, not at the bulky forms of the mutineers standing right over them. But around them. Behind them. The menacing growls, only a component of the night's earlier ensemble, now sounded loud and immediate, as if they had closed in the distance from the endless plain to the edge of the escarpment to become the primary instrument of the Arenes nocturnal symphony.

Heike was trembling fearfully and Leyn began to sense the strained tension in the air.

Bastiaansz and the other mutineer drifted into his focus. They stood, frozen, looking around them fearfully, seemingly oblivious to Leyn and Heike helpless at their feet.

The growls were filled with fierce warning. Shadows surrounded the small group of the four shipwreck survivors.

Shadows that stalked and circled. Shadows that grinned to display ferocious gleaming teeth.

Leyn wondered if he was dead after all. Not able to place the presence of those shadows with their predatory grins into the context of real life.

"*Was zum Teufel*[22] are those things?" Heike asked with terror in her tone.

"Duvelsbeesten," Bastiaansz answered Heike's question. Stunned into fright, he sounded almost civil. "Devil's beasts."

Heike shuddered.

Leyn's conviction that he had passed from the realm of the living became stronger when the shadows took on distinctive but surreal appearances.

They were huge and hairy, with short stubby snouts from which protruded evil looking 'V' shaped teeth, small, rounded ears, and sinister eyes that glowed like amber. Their broad paws ended in powerful claws, with enlarged hooked thumb claws. They exuded a primal menace.

Like demons! We're in a nightmare and will wake up soon.

"It'll be alright," Leyn assured Heike.

The reverberations of the night's continuous din died away as if in hushed expectation, leaving just the bestial snarls of anger. Only the cicadas continued their high-pitched trilling, apparently unconcerned by the otherwise all-encompassing menace that had filled the night.

Some of the duvelsbeesten stopped prowling, rising on their hind legs instead, appearing to use their tails as extra appendage for balance, as the beasts closed in on the mutineers.

------

[22] *Was zum Teufel* – German for 'What the Devil'

A few, still on all fours, crept closer to Leyn and Heike, sniffing tentatively.

It was beginning to feel a bit too real for Leyn when the duvelsbeest closest to him thrust its head forward. The foul hotness of its breath brushed against Leyn's cheeks and assaulted his nose. The beast pushed its hideous head closer. Leyn pulled his head away until he bumped against Heike's head. She was similarly recoiling from a duvelsbeest's intrusive snout. Leyn could now see long blade-like teeth deeper in their mouths, half hidden by the creatures' cheeks.

The duvelsbeesten stopped to raise their heads and utter fierce roars.

Leyn and Heike clutched hands tightly.

21. Lost and Found

Arenes, Western Australia, 2016

Supplied with a firm date, Lette hit her laptop and worked through the rest of the day, most of the night, and much of the next morning. The others let her be, other than occasionally bringing her a cup of tea, food, or the admonition that she had to get some sleep at least. She missed the return of the rest of the shoreline platform crew and the triumph with which boxes full of silver coins had been carried into camp like the spoils of war.

After Lette was satisfied that she could present a decent set of preliminary findings she consulted with Penning.

"Can you make a quick PowerPoint?" Penning asked.

"There's a beamer?"

"I'll have one of the techies set it up in the Sea Dog's Cabin," Penning said. "Nice and dark in there, and the tent with the least finds, so we should be able to set up chairs from the mess tent."

Lette had intended to quickly guide the crew through her PowerPoint, but Penning wasn't having any of that.

"Drama! Flair! These people deserve a performance, Lette. It's what they have worked so hard for. They've found the bones. You're about to add flesh to those bones. Don't underestimate how important this is for the dig. I've got an idea!"

And so it came to be that the crew at Camp Whoop Whoop stopped whatever they were doing when the camp's loudspeakers burst into the call for equality, freedom, and brotherhood presented by the fourth movement of Beethoven's Ninth Symphony. The rousing choral of *Ode to Joy* was totally out of place here where the dusty escarpment of Arenes fell to meet the thunderous waves of the Indian Ocean, yet somehow oddly appropriate.

> *Joyful, joyful, we adore Thee*
> *God of glory, Lord of love;*
> *Hearts unfold like flowers afore Thee*
> *Opening to the sun above.*
> *Melt the clouds of sin and sadness,*
> *Drive the dark of doubt away;*
> *Giver of immortal gladness*
> *Fill us with the light of day!*

People drifted to the Sea Dog's Cabin from all over the camp, many singing, or at least humming along. The expectation on their faces was unnerving and it was only Penning's encouraging nods that kept Lette from running all the way to Maroons Cove as quickly as she could.

> *All Thy works with joy surround Thee,*
> *Earth and heaven reflect Thy rays,*
> *Stars and angels sing around Thee,*
> *Centre of unbroken praise;*
> *Field and forest, vale and mountain,*
> *Flowery meadow, flashing sea,*

Singing bird and flowing fountain
Call us to rejoice in Thee.

There were no lights on in the Sea Dog's Cabin, other than the flicker from the beamer lens as it projected the first slide upon a screen. The dates had gone around the camp like wildfire, of course, but there was something special about seeing them in print. They formed the entirety of the first slide that Lette had hastily prepared.

1615-1616

When all were seated, Penning announced, "Having set entirely reasonable expectations with our little song, I would like to invite Miss Lette Sabajo to 'lift us to the joy divine'."

The audience cheered and Penning threw Lette a mean grin. Lette knew about Penning's reputation for making life hard for the students whom she supervised, but had had no idea that it would have included a situation like this. However, it was also a challenge of sorts, Lette reckoned. A reminder that Lette had better get used to this if she wanted to progress in the field, and that notion filled Lette with the courage she needed. That and Penning's earlier reminder that the Whoop Whoop crew had been working hard for weeks and deserved a reward for their efforts.

Just focus on the context, not all the staring and expectant eyes.

"Thank you, Professor Penning," Lette started. "Now as you may know, I started my archive search using 'Arenes' as search term and this yielded very little. It confirmed that VOC captains marooned condemned crew members at Maroons Cove on occasion, and it confirmed that a VOC ship was wrecked on Arenes. A very specific number was given regarding the people who lost their lives in that wreck, namely 193 in total, which suggests that someone survived the shipwreck to convey this information. Unfortunately, the primary document regarding this has only survived in fragmentary condition, leaving us with partial hints as to the date survivors were found, and the captain and ship involved in the rescue." She clicked for the next slide.

16...

Skipper Ha...
VOC ship *De B...*

"The incredible discovery made in the blowhole yesterday has given us a concrete date to work with."

Lette clicked the next slide that showed a photograph of silver coins resting in water in the conservation tent. The coins were all the same, and their date of minting was clear to see on most of them: 1615.

"These coins bear the hallmark of the Middelburg Mint," Lette continued. "The records of the Middelburg Mint have survived in excellent state and from them I was able to discover that the 1615 production of coins was designated in its entirety for transport to the East Indies. The coins were distributed between the ships of the 1615 autumn fleet. Every single one of those ships made it to Batavia, barring one…"

She paused and was pleased to note that her audience seemed to hold its collective breath. It stood to reason that the missing ship was missing no more, its remnants surrounding them here in this tent on the edge of the world, or else scattered on the seabed by the reefs below. Lette clicked for the next slide.

De Armuyden

There were excited murmurs and cheers. The nameless wreck had just become something much more. It had been given an identity. It was unspoken as of yet, but Camp Whoop Whoop had just become Camp Armuyden, the nameless cliffs the Armuyden Cliffs, and the famous four would now undoubtedly become the famous five.

"Next, I searched for all likely ships with names that started with a 'B' which might have been in this vicinity in 1615, or, considering the length of the journey and the as of yet unknown period of time that survivors stayed here on Arenes, 1616 and 1617. I found a very likely candidate, but the name of the skipper provided a bit of a puzzle. The ship in question was captained by one Hendrick van der Dekken when it departed Holland. Now as I'm sure you all know, the 17th and 18th century Dutch liked to spell everything in at least three or four different ways just to confound the Western Australian Museum many years later…"

There was much laughter at that. Penning nodded approvingly.

"But I've personally never encountered the name Hendrik spelled with an 'a', so 'Handrick van der Dekken', although I couldn't dismiss the possibility entirely, seemed unlikely. However, having the name of the ship allowed me to discover that Hendrick van der Dekken died during a storm at Cape Agulhas, and was replaced by his First Mate, one Peter Haelen, giving us our 'Skipper Ha…'. Interestingly, this ship was part of the same fleet that *De Armuyden* was part of.

"Of course, once a fleet had rounded the Cape of Good Hope, having sailed down the Atlantic in convoy for protection, it was every captain for himself, and it became a bit of a race to reach Batavia before the others. We now know the date that Haelen reached Arenes and found *Armuyden* survivors, but it still remains unclear exactly how many days, weeks, or months the shipwreck survivors were stranded here. What we can deduce, is that any passing ship would have been a chance encounter. Any fears the survivors might have had that it would be years before they were found - if ever – were realistic but needless. They were very lucky in that respect. Anyhow, I now had much more information to base searches on…" Lette clicked for the next slide.

23 September 1616

Skipper Peter Haelen

VOC ship *De Blokzeyl*

"Haelen made it somewhat difficult for me as he duly logged his encounter with *De Armuyden* survivors but made no specific mention of Arenes." Lette clicked for the next slide.

Bij het passeren van een eiland nabij de westkust van het Zuidland, zagen wij sporen van een vergaan schip. Middels rook signalen bovenaan een klip, verwittigden overlevenden ons betreffende hun aanwezigheid. Het schip genaamd De Armuyden was onderdeel van onze herfstvloot. Slechts twintig gezellen hebben de ramp overleefd. 193 zielen zijn verloren, alsmede de inboedel van De Armuyden. Duiken was door omstandigheden levensgevaarlijk. Geen officieren behoorden tot de overlevenden. Het bevel was over-genomen door een onderofficier, de scheepsarts Niklas

Zonvelt, mij welbekend. Zonvelt verklaarde dat een deel van de overlevende gezellen tot muiterij waren overgegaan, maar al reeds met hun leven hadden betaald voor deze zware en onvergeeflijke overtreding.

"I assume you all speak Dutch by now?" Lette asked, drawing laughter.

"*Wij wel hoor*[23]!" One of the Dutch crew answered.

"It's a bit rusty, best translate," Fieldman replied.

"What you don't see here is the left column of *De Blokzeyl's* log, where Haelen notes the date – the 23rd of September 1616 –, his course – north by northwest on a broad reach –, his latitude, and his estimated longitude. The latter is surprisingly accurate, but if they had sighted the Australian coast they would have had a good idea where they were. Then comes the entry you see on the slide. It's fairly long, presumably because he would have been expected to deliver a full report to the VOC when he reached Batavia."

Lette paused for a breath. "It translates as follows: '*While we passed an island close to the west coast of the Southland we saw traces of a shipwreck.*'

"This could mean there was a lot of wreckage to be seen on the shoreline platform, or possibly intact parts of the hull that hadn't fully submerged yet. Both would indicate that the wreck was still relatively recent. Haelen

---

[23] We do!

then adds that the survivors lit a beacon signal on top of the cliffs to draw *De Blokzeyl's* attention."

"We found evidence of a large fire on top of the larger cave," Penning contributed.

"A convergence then, of a primary document and the archaeology. Haelen continues, naming the ship as *De Armuyden* and mentioning that it was part of 'our' autumn fleet. He reports that only twenty people survived the disaster, and that 193 souls were lost, as well as the cargo. Note that, in contrast to that later VOC record, he places crew before cargo."

"Heresy!" Bruce called out, drawing a few laughs.

"That's followed by the sentence: *'Circumstances made diving life-threatening.'* I suspect that this is because the VOC would have expected Haelen to do everything in his power to recover the coin chests.

"Skipper Haelen should have crawled down a blowhole," Fieldman joked. "But probably wasn't mad as a gum tree full of galahs[24] like our Bruce."

"I protest!" Bruce called out over the laughter that followed Fieldman's jest.

Lette smiled and waited for her audience to become silent again, which was soon enough as they were riveted to the presentation. "The next bit is interesting and gives us a name. Haelen writes: *'None of the senior officers survived. Command had been assumed by a junior officer, the ship's surgeon, Niklas Zonvelt.'*"

---

[24] An Australian type of cockatoo that lives in large and noisy flocks

There was a collective sigh, as it was always a pleasure and often a luxury to be able to name some of those involved at the time.

"If he was the ship's surgeon then Niklas Zonvelt would have been the one who had so skilfully reset the broken bones," Bruce said.

"I would presume so," Lette agreed. "Haelen also adds that he was acquainted with Zonvelt, which isn't necessarily a surprise as the world of *Oostvaarders*, those who went on these early voyages East, was a small one. The last part of the entry is fascinating, as I think it will help us understand at least part of the puzzle of the various burials. Haelen writes: '*Zonvelt declared that some of the survivors had taken to mutiny but had already paid for this transgression with their lives.*'"

There was an immediate buzz of comments and rapid consultation as this was digested. Lette had expected this, so was content to wait until the immediate impact of that news died down.

"That certainly deserves renewed analysis then," Fieldman said, clearly pleased.

Lette nodded,

Lette continued, "I'm afraid that this presentation only covers my preliminary findings. With all the new information now uncovered, I'll have a lot of work on my plate over the next few weeks."

"Optimist!" Penning called out. "Months, years even. Just you wait."

Lette grinned. "I look forward to it. There are, however, two more findings I'd like to share with you now, revealing some more names and throwing some light on other question marks raised by your work."

22. Gory Banquet

Arenes, The Southland, 1616

Leyn turned his face away when the duvelsbeest closest to him looked back down and revealed a slobbering tongue.

The stinky breath washed over Leyn's face again. The duvelsbeest's long tongue slithered out and lathered Leyn's cheek, moist with the texture of a rough sponge. It left a trail of slime.

"Ugh," Heike said, receiving a similar treatment.

Leyn shook his head in disbelief when the duvelsbeest backed off, as if having lost all interest in him.

It isn't going to eat me?

He turned to see Heike struck by incredulity as well.

The mutineers weren't as lucky.

The creatures shoved Bastiaansz and the other mutineer onto the ground, gripping their shoulders between their large front teeth and using their thumb claws to rend open the men's abdomens.

The mutineers screamed in agony at the pain, which only became worse when the beasts used their paws to pin the men's chests and legs down, and sank their teeth into the now exposed innards, to tear out the guts and start gnawing on them. They grunted contentedly over their meal, occasionally snarling at one another as warning to stay clear, and apparently wholly unconcerned about the fact that their meals thrashed in desperation and shrieked loudly.

Bastiaansz screamed more shrilly than the little girl he had casually punched out. Leyn felt little sympathy as he watched, heard, and smelled the gruesome duvelsbeesten's gory banquet unfold, knowing that an alternative scenario would have been the human beasts having their way with Heike. The sight he saw now was nauseating but he couldn't tear his eyes away until Bastiaansz and his companion stopped screaming and died.

As if disinterested in meat that didn't pulse with life, the beasts abandoned their meal and loped off to the cave, leaving the grisly remnants of their supper sprawled out on the bloodied ground.

Howls, roars, and terrified screams filled the cave.

Leyn and Heike looked at each other.

"Do you think that…?"

"Let's go see," They got to their feet, slowly, painfully, supporting each other, and then limped to the cave, stopping within view of the entrance.

23. Liselotte's Journal

Arenes, Western Australia, 2016

Lette clicked for the next slide.

Liselotte Haelen's Journal, 1623

"The first extra finding that I'd like to share now is a journal entry from 1623, kept in the archives of the Rotterdam Museum. It seems that Peter Haelen was back in the East Indies in 1623, this time as captain of a ship called *De Christine*, which was not a VOC ship but registered as an independent trader. An oddity at a time when the stranglehold of the VOC monopoly had been well established.

"The journal was kept by one Liselotte Haelen, a cousin of Peter Haelen, but the journal is incomplete, so I don't know why she was in the Indies or what she was doing on *De Christine*. The following entry was made when *De Christine* anchored at Amboyna."

Lette clicked for the next slide, which consisted of another Dutch text, in neat and steady cursive handwriting. "The translation is as follows: '*Niklas took us to see some friends of his today. They were shipmates of his on De Armuyden and they were shipwrecked together off the New Holland coast about seven years ago. They were my age then, now in their early twenties. Niklas made disapproving comments about how they couldn't keep their hands off each other on the island they were stranded on, but it's quite clear to me that he's very fond of them. The man is called Leyn Jonas, and his wife Heike.'"*

Lette paused again in acknowledgement of how meaningful actual names were in that they provided human individuality to the otherwise silent witnesses formed by lifeless artifacts. The discovery had certainly triggered her imagination, knowing now that the large cave had been inhabited by a ship's surgeon called Niklas Zonvelt, and a young couple who had managed to pursue romance amidst all the misery and madness.

"Liselotte Haelen continues, mentioning that *'Leyn works as a VOC clerk at the castle now.'*

"Seeing that this visit took place on Amboyna, that 'castle' she refers to would be Fort Victoria, which served as VOC HQ in the Maluku islands.

"There's more in the journal that's relevant for us: *'They are very kind people and had many memories to recall with Niklas, but I think there are things they avoid talking about. There were a lot of meaningful glances and abrupt changes in topic. Heike and Leyn have a gorgeous toddler, a happy little boy, whom they have called Rykert. This after a Boatswain on De Armuyden who was killed by mutineers on the island. Leyn was much taken by this Rykert. His description reminds me of Walter. A very big man, but apparently Rykert had a damaged face, with a broken nose and a scar that ran from his eyebrow to his cheek. Leyn said that Rykert was tough but with a heart of gold.'"*

"Was that facial scar diagonal or vertical?" Bruce asked.

"That's not mentioned, I'm afraid."

"We've got an individual in The Morgue who matches that description though," Bruce said with excitement. "Much larger than average, with a broken nose, and traces of a diagonal blade furrow from the left forehead to the right chin, healed, so predating his death. He was killed by two gun shots."

"That is probably Rykert then," Lette said. "This was the end of Liselotte Haelen's relevant entry, but I did a quick search and confirmed that a man called Koos Rykert, from Alkmaar in North Holland, was mustered on *De Armuyden* as boatswain. There was also mention of a VOC soldier, or mercenary if you will, from Germany called Bertram Steenbeck and a reference to his sister Heike Steenbeck who accompanied him on the voyage. The 'Walter' Liselotte Haelen refers to was possibly Walter Zundert, who was Second Mate on *De Christine*."

"Absolutely fascinating," Penning commented. "You said there was another record you wanted to share."

"Indeed," Lette confirmed, and clicked on the next slide.

From Steyn Florentin's Observations (1619)

"Many of you may already be aware that Steyn Florentin was a physician in Batavia who did groundbreaking pioneer work in the field of tropical medicine. He wrote a book on his findings, *An Account of the Diseases, Natural History and Medicines of the East Indies* that was published posthumously in 1631. It was translated into English in 1769. One part of that book was headed 'Observations', in which Florentin describes various cases that he thought were particularly interesting. Relevant to us is Observation Thirteen. I will let you read it for yourself."

Lette showed them the next slide.

Obſerv.XIII Of a perſon who died of a Malady of the Mind

In 1619 one Willem Duyt was brought to us in a ſtate of conſiderable diſtress. Being a former ſhipmate of a particular friend of mine, ſurgeon Zonvelt, I took a perſonal intereſt. Duyt complained that he was unable to ſleep, nor reſt becauſe the mereſt ſound or ſudden movement would reſult in his deſire to run away, or freeze in terror, or react with violence which ſaw him get into regular trouble. At other times he ſaid he would feel nothing at all (in general), finding himſelf entirely numb and without energy. He ſaid he found no more pleaſure in drinking or companionſhip, though ſometime would take to the bottle in order to forget but could not tell me what he wanted to forget. I teſted him for all manner of phyſical ailments but found nothing, nor did any of the phyſical remedies we tried cauſe any change. Duyt was an Armuyden ſurvivor and as I was the phyſician in charge of examining all thoſe who ſurvived that shipwreck upon their arrival in Batavia, I had at that time noted a collective reluctance to ſpeak much about what they had experienced, even my friend Zonvelt. The condition of Duyt worſened and I believe he began to relive events of the paſt, ever more vividly, ſo I thought I would find out more, but any rational account always quickly developed into the ravings of a deluſional lunatic. He would ſcream about giant apes with long tails, or of a lion-bear with beaver teeth come to eat him. Theſe creatures and the danger they poſed became real enough to his mind that, unfortunately and deſpite precautions we put in place, Duyt took his own life.

"Jesus wept!" Bruce exclaimed when he had finished reading.

"Classic PTSD," Fieldman said. "The denial of what he thought was ever so real must have snapped something in him."

"That poor man," Penning commiserated.

"I thought the references to 'giant apes with long tails' and 'lion-bears with beaver teeth' were particularly apt," Lette said.

There were many nods.

134

"If only to remind us to be very careful with releasing information," Fieldman told the entire audience sternly. "We must keep the museum's reputation in mind."

"Anyhow, that's all I have to report for now," Lette concluded her presentation.

Penning began to clap. "Bravo!"

The others rose as well, shouting their approval and clapping their hands. Lette beamed, but reckoned the applause was in acknowledgement of much more than her simple presentation. The crew, having spent weeks working hard in the heat and dust, were applauding their own efforts as well, and celebrating the way their finds had become so much more alive now that some of the background story was known. And perhaps – and wouldn't that be most fitting? – they were applauding the human beings who had lived and died here four hundred years ago: Niklas Zonvelt, Leyn Jonas, Bertram and Heike Steenbeck, Koos Rykert, and Willem Duyt.

When the applause finally died down, to be replaced by the hum of conversation, Lette was approached by Penning and Fieldman, both of whom insisted on shaking her hand.

"Splendid work," Penning said. "I really hope that you'll take my proposal into serious consideration, Lette."

"I've thought about it, and the answer is 'yes' and 'thank you'," Lette told her, much to Penning's visible delight.

"Well that was…" Fieldman began to say but was interrupted by a sudden unexpected sound from the tent next to them. All talk faded as people looked up in surprise and shock. There was a series of long growling grunts from the Landlubber's HQ, like a grumpy warning, low in pitch and seeming to reverberate ominously. Then came the sound of a table crashing over and the patter of finds on the floor.

Bruce spoke for all of them when he exclaimed, "What the hell…!"

24. Grim Work

Arenes, The Southland, 1616

The duvelsbeesten didn't tarry in the cave for long. They soon came out, each dragging a struggling, shouting or screaming mutineer over the ground. The captives were yanked and lugged to the saddle, and then down to the plains. It was there that the shrieking began in earnest, muted by distance but remaining audible for some time.

Leyn and Heike barely registered the distant screams of the mutineers, fully occupied as they were in the cave, sorting the living from the dead. None of the survivors of the mutineers' attack had suffered from the attentions of the beasts, though many had been murdered or grievously wounded by Bastiaansz's rogues, including the two German women who had suffered other attentions as well.

They found Niklas relatively unscathed. The old tar quickly took charge, organising those who could get on their feet in the care of those who couldn't. Willem Duyt had survived as well. He'd been knocked out by a blow to the head when the mutineers had dispatched Rykert's surviving men. They had presumed he was dead and left him be.

Leyn and Heike went to look for the small German children knocked out by Bastiaanz and found them, dazed with aching heads, but alive. They took the children back to the cave, where Willem voiced a fear felt by most, "What if those duvelsbeesten come back?"

Niklas nodded. "A justified question. To be entirely honest, I don't think they will. But it would help, I suspect, if we refrained from shooting at any wildlife. We've got enough bread, even some salted meat, and will stick to that diet."

"That doesn't make sense," Willem noted. "Why would a duvelsbeest care if we hunted other game?"

Niklas shrugged. "Maybe they don't like the competition? I'm not sure Willem. It's just a strong feeling I have."

Leyn, recalling how the duvelsbeesten had inspected both Heike and him before letting them be and had been highly selective in choosing their prey in the cave, reckoned that Niklas was right.

It was close to dawn when they collapsed into an exhausted sleep. Niklas had them up by noon again, announcing that it was time for the grim task of burying the dead. He was concerned about the heat and said the work couldn't wait unless they all wanted to get ill or attract the unwanted attentions of whatever carrion beasts might reside on Arenes.

They considered piling up the bodies in one of the further caves and sealing that up, but in the end the ship's surgeon decided that with the sheer number of corpses this too might become a health hazard. There was a relatively clear patch of sandy soil some way to the east of the main cave, where they dug forty graves and a mass grave for the mutineers who had perished around the cave. This work wasn't finished until the day after, when they could at last lay the dead to rest, with a short collective prayer spoken by

Niklas. After the others had returned to the cave to prepare a simple meal, Leyn hovered by Rykert's grave a while longer to say a private goodbye to the bane of ship's boys whom he had come to appreciate a great deal.

25. Oh *Mi Gado*

Arenes, Western Australia, 2016

There was a mad dash to the Landlubber's HQ.

Two large birds were perched upon the roof. In appearance they looked like female pheasants but were much larger. Their feathers were various hues of brown, some speckled, and they had red throat markings. Most remarkable though, were their tails, with a long, elegantly curved tail that was evenly striped in dark brown and beige colours and accompanied by long spindly silver tail feathers that gave the impression of lyres.

"Lyrebirds," Penning exclaimed. "Were they making those sounds?"

As in answer, the deep throaty rumbling growls sounded from within the tent again. The sounds stopped abruptly when the front tent flaps were swept open by many hands.

Mouths dropped open, or else uttered expletives or expressions of disbelief that were immediately echoed by the lyrebirds.

Inside the crew of Camp Armuyden saw a gigantic bipedal creature, so tall that its head brushed against the top of the tent. It stood on muscular legs that curved out of humongous buttocks, as did a sturdy tapered tail that rested on the ground. The creature's upper body was immensely muscled, with a chest and arms that appeared to mimic human physiology. The creature's head had a well-defined chin, short-snubbed snout and forward-facing eyes that gave it the appearance of a sentient being that might start speaking to them any moment.

Instead, it uttered more of those deep guttural growls, a clear warning to leave it be.

"Good God," Fieldman said, flabbergasted.

Lette shared his astonishment. This could be nothing other than one of the procoptodon goliahs they had discussed at length.

Bruce said nothing for a change, instead turning abruptly to rush to one of the smaller office tents.

"Keep clear of it," Penning called out. "Better yet, back off some. Leave the tent entrance clear."

A few folks shuffled back a little, but most were rooted to the spot, staring at the goliah in amazement.

The goliah growled again and took a few lumbering steps forward, raising its arms in a classic boxer's pose. The meaning of that was abundantly clear.

"For fuck's sake," Penning shouted. "This is a wild animal. Back off, give it space."

This time, the urgency in her voice and the clear hostility displayed by the goliah resulted in a slow collective retreat, though none took their eyes off the impossible sight of the giant kangaroo.

The goliah snorted, but not in triumph, Lette reckoned, as it turned its head this way and that, as if seeking an escape route.

"It's scared," Lette concluded.

"Wouldn't you be?" Penning asked sharply.

As if to demonstrate the opposite, the goliah strode to one of the finds tables and gave it a mighty kick with one of its legs. The table promptly succumbed and fell sideways, spilling the finds. A wine glass that had survived a shipwreck and remained intact for four hundred years shattered into pieces, startling the goliah who growled a deep warning at the source of the sound.

"Goddamn it, it's destroying our bloody finds," one of the men near Lette grumbled.

"Goddamn it," one of the lyrebirds replied.

The other lyrebird uttered a near-perfect imitation of the sound of shattering glass.

Bruce returned, carrying a rifle in his hands.

"Bruce, no," Fieldman said.

"You can't just shoot it!" Lette exclaimed. For an irrational moment she intended to tell him that the goliah was surely a protected species, until she realised that even a fanatic government bureaucrat was unlikely to issue a declaration of protection for an animal that was deemed to have stopped existing more than ten thousand years ago.

"Why not?" Bruce growled. "Bloody roos are pests. Destroy our farms, now destroy our priceless finds."

"Bruce," Penning said sternly. "Don't you realise what a unique anomaly this is? That's even more priceless than a wine glass, surely."

"Vermin," Bruce spat out, starting to walk toward the tent entrance that they had all just vacated.

The goliah stared at him, seeming to recognise the hostile intent. It threw its head backward and uttered a primal scream of anger.

Inside the crew of Camp Armuyden saw a gigantic bipedal creature, so tall that its head brushed against the top of the tent.
(Illustration by Tom Brown)

"Yeah, fuck you too, roo." Bruce raised his rifle.

The goliah lowered its head again and began to march forward, swinging its powerful fore arms in mock punches and growling mightily.

The rifle cracked loudly, stopping the goliah in its track. It looked down at the growing bloodstain on its chest with an almost human expression of surprise and then wailed in agony.

"*Godverdomme*[25]," Penning shook her head in dismay. "Men."

The goliah slowly toppled over, but wasn't dead, mewling piteously now, staring at them in helpless agony, its great legs twitching feebly. Lette thought her heart would break at the sight of its anguish.

The lyrebirds, clearly inspired, began producing rifle shot sounds, primal screams, growls, and mewling.

"For God's sake man," Fieldman snarled at Bruce. "Release it from its misery. Finish what you started."

Bruce, however, seemed to realise the magnitude of his action and lowered the rifle, shaking his head with a stunned expression on his face.

The goliah continued to mewl, sounding almost like a crying child.

Cursing, Fieldman grabbed the rifle from Bruce's hands, cocked it, and then delivered the mercy shot, ending the goliah's mortal agony.

This time the shot seemed to disturb the lyrebirds, who lifted off the tent roof clumsily, winging away on their

---

[25] Dutch for 'God damn it'

short wings, though continuing to mimic the sounds of the drama they had just witnessed.

The humans all stood in stunned silence. Nobody spoke.

Shaking his head, Fieldman quietly lowered the tent flaps to conceal the sight of the dead goliah. That stirred some into action, walking away in silence.

The earlier mood of elation and excitement at the new discoveries had waned entirely. The evening meal was eaten in silence. Nobody felt much like singing or bantering around campfires, withdrawing into their tents early instead, Lette included.

To make it worse, the lyrebirds had spread their mimicry across the plain, with other lyrebirds picking it up. Lette heard the goliah's growls, the sharp crack of the rifle, and wails of pain again and again. The Kookaburras and Curlews added manic laughter and screams of distress to the whole, as if the whole plain was traumatised and reliving the bloody scene at the Landlubber's HQ continuously.

Lette crawled into her sleeping bag and curled up, pressing her hands to her ears. "Make it stop," she whispered. "Please make it stop."

Trying to block out the sounds, it took some time for her to register the addition of new sounds. Low growls. Different from those of the goliah, far more menacing, far more deadly, far more capable of inspiring primeval terror.

It wasn't until she saw the walls of her tent bend inward some, as if something was prowling outside of it, and then heard a woman scream, that Lette realised their nightmare had intensified.

"Stay in your tents! Stay in your tents!" Penning's voice sounded loud and clear.

Lette stared, wide-eyed, at a new indentation of the canvas wall of her tent, as if someone …something was pressing its snout against it. Lette's heart pounded away as she heard it sniff, cautiously at first, but then much more intently, as if trying to establish who was inside.

Mi gado mi gado mi gado mi gado mi gado mi gado[26]

The creature snorted before uttering a curt growl and backing off. Had it gone? If it was walking away, it did so with such stealth that Lette couldn't discern the movement. She tried to crawl deeper into the false sense of security offered by her sleeping bag.

Mi gado mi gado mi gado mi gado mi gado mi gado

Seconds…minutes…hours later, Lette couldn't tell, there were sudden snarls, the sound of ripping canvas, a man's shouts of horror and then screams of pain. The sound was repeated from another corner of the camp. It seemed that the attackers, multiple in number, converged on those two scenes of terror for a group effort, roaring in fury now, though that didn't overpower the desperate screams of human anguish.

Mi gado mi gado mi gado mi gado mi gado mi gado

The unholy combination of snarls, roars, and screams diminished, and then faded into the distance as the creatures dragged their victims into the bush. Lette waited

---

[26] 'my god' in Sranantongo (Sranan), the informal language of Surinam.

in fear and trepidation for their return. She could hear sobbing and hyperventilated breathing from the tents nearest to her, the occupants experiencing the same numbing dread that overwhelmed Lette.

Lette didn't sleep a wink that night, nor did she dare brave the darkness. It wasn't until dawn that she emerged from her tent warily, ready to run, but the camp looked oddly peaceful other than two tents the shredded canvas of which turned and twitched slowly in the morning breeze.

Penning, pale and grim, held a muster at the mess tent. Bruce and Martin Fieldman were missing. Search parties were organized, the available rifles in the camp divided between them. There were no signs of the stealthy killers that had infiltrated the camp, but an increasing number of black-breasted buzzards gliding low over a particular spot just a mile or so from the camp signaled a potential ground zero.

They found Bruce and Fieldman there, or, what remained of them, their mutilated corpses already crawling with meat ants. In case the humans couldn't quite comprehend what had occurred here, lyrebirds helpfully replayed a gruesome soundtrack of shrieks, snarls, growls, roars, ripping flesh, and breaking bones. All but one, which had learned another trick, joyfully singing snatches of Beethoven to add to the auditory mayhem.

Ever singing, march we onward, victors in the midst of strife.

26. A Promise to Fulfil

Arenes, The Southland, 1616

Settling into their new abode at last, the remaining survivors soon discovered that the caves weren't the only cavities of interest to them. Upon closer inspection of the gullies and rocky crevices of the plain around the clifftop caves they discovered a great many small pits, natural cisterns that had collected and retained rainwater. Vital to their continued ability to survive these discoveries were greeted with relief.

Leyn and Heike took it upon themselves to continue exploring their new environment, venturing ever further from the basecamp in the large cave. They were somewhat apprehensive at first, fearing a return of the duvelsbeesten, but as the days passed became increasingly convinced that their initial encounter with the creatures evidenced a peculiar tendency of the predators to be highly selective in choosing their meals. Though Leyn and Heike remained wary and never strayed too far from the cliff edges, they grew more confident with every exploration they completed.

On their third outing Leyn spotted a great many tracks on the sandy patches between the scattered low brush. All seemed to indicate a regular migration to and from a narrow cave entrance, not much more than a fissure in the rock face.

"No pawprints of larger animals," Heike noted with relief that was shared by Leyn.

"Those fat-tailed apes and duvelsbeesten wouldn't fit," Leyn indicated the narrow dark gap. "You and I could probably only just squeeze through."

"We ought to," Heike decided.

"You reckon?"

"Well, there's something in there, has to be. Why else would so many animals go in there?"

Leyn shrugged, having rapidly learned to dislike or at the very least distrust Arenes wildlife. "To sharpen vicious little teeth on a rock?" he suggested. "The better to eat us with?"

Heike responded with a wry grin. "Could be, but it could also be water. We need to find out."

Leyn relented. Finding water sources, after all, was the primary goal of these expeditions, slightly more imperative than drinking in the sight of Heike and relishing her company out of sight of the others.

At first, as they took turns squeezing through the narrow cave entrance, Leyn reckoned that they'd just find themselves fumbling in the dark through an ever-narrowing passage, but the ingress widened into a large rectangular cavern. The roof was honeycombed with irregular gaps through which beams of sunlight descended to form golden columns of light.

"*Gott im Himmel*!"[27] Heike exclaimed in wonder when she saw the light dancing over the glittering surface of a

---

[27] Literally 'God in heaven' in German, used as 'good heavens' or 'oh my God'.

large pool of water that occupied most of the cavernous chamber.

A slightly downward curving slope of sand led to the edge of the pool, pockmarked by a multitude of animal and bird prints. Here and there were small piles of droppings, clumps of fur, and discarded feathers.

The air in the cavern was cool, sweet, and soothing in contrast to the dry and dusty air outside.

"A lot better than the small cisterns of rainwater we've been finding," Leyn said. "Niklas will be well pleased."

"*Stimmt,*"[28] Heike agreed, albeit with a reluctant tone. She brightened. "But right now, this is our secret."

She glided closer to Leyn, a mischievous smile accompanied by a sudden bright twinkle in her eyes. Raising a hand, she brushed her fingers along his cheek.

Startled by the sudden intimacy, Leyn wasn't sure how to respond.

"I wonder," Heike murmured. "I wonder what you look like, beneath all this grime."

"Huh? Much the same, I should think."

"Puh. Dutch barbarian." Heike shook her head. "You're filthy, we're both covered in dust and dirt."

She scrunched her nose. "And we both smell foul."

"You smell lovely," Leyn lied.

"*Quatsch!* But we can remedy that now, can't we?"

"Remedy?" Leyn asked.

"You really don't know much," Heike tutted. By way of further explanation, she fumbled at the remnants of her

---

28 German for 'agreed' or 'that's right'

battered shift and let it flutter down until it sank on the sand around her feet.

Leyn's mouth fell open as he stared wide-eyed at her curvaceous nudity, finally realising what Heike had been hinting at.

"It's more awkward, you know, if you don't undress too," Heike admonished him.

Aware that his growing arousal was as of yet somewhat concealed by his breeches, Leyn coloured red and stammered, "But, but Heike…"

Stepping closer, Heike murmured, "We made each other a promise not long ago, didn't we? In the moonlight?"

Leyn nodded.

"You wanted to kiss me then," Heike reminded him, quite needlessly. She added, with feigned innocence. "You no longer wish to?"

"Of course I do," Leyn protested fervently.

"Well then," she said, "It's time to fulfil that promise."

Leyn concurred and did as he was told. Soon after the cavern was filled with splashing and laughter as the two washed off all the horror of preceding days, as well as layers of Arenes dust. And after that? Suffice to say that the chamber was permeated by other sounds, starting with soft gasps of pleasure and ending in a passionate clamour.

27. The Usual Suspects

Arenes, Western Australia, 2016

Some of the crew wanted to bury the remains of Bruce and Fieldman but Penning immediately vetoed that.

"We have to report these deaths to the AFP[29] asap. We'll tell them what we know but place yourself in their shoes. Would you believe wild tales about prehistoric kangaroos and lions if you hadn't seen or heard such anomalies yourself? They will treat this as suspicious, mark my words. I'm truly sorry about what happened to Martin and Bruce and would like nothing better than to lay them to rest. But we will treat this area as a crime scene. To be left untouched for the police to investigate. You're all trained to avoid contamination of a site; I'd ask you to put that professionalism into practice."

There were nods of agreement. Lette noticed that nobody questioned Penning's assumption of Fieldman's authority. She herself was amazed by Penning's ability to focus on practical manners when most, like Lette herself, seemed overwhelmed by the horror of it all and grief for their deceased colleagues.

"What do we do?" somebody asked.

"The AFP are likely to want to question all of us," Penning answered. "Like it or not, but for the time-being we're all potential suspects in what they might view as a

---

[29] Australian Federal Police

murder case. I need to report to the museum as well. I suspect they'll shut the camp down."

There were moans and groans at that.

"I know," Penning said curtly. "We'll be here for a week yet, I suspect, if not longer.. I would fully understand if any of you chose not to, but I suggest we make the most of that remaining week. In short, we go back to work while we can. If only to occupy our minds."

"What if those beasts come back?" the conservation tent technician asked nervously.

Penning took a deep breath. "That's been on my mind too. It might help if we transform the storage containers into temporary sleeping quarters. It'll be tight, but at least we'll be able to lock up for the night and be safe. Though I suspect it'll also help if we don't start taking pot shots if another goliah shows up."

Lette nodded. She had been thinking about the precision with which the predators had selected their victims, the same men who had fired a rifle at the goliah, even though Fieldman had done so out of compassion. She was glad Penning had hinted at it, because while it appeared logical on one hand, it was entirely insane when you thought about it. That degree of sentient thinking? The ability to sniff out the shooters? It made no sense whatsoever. Then again, neither did the continued existence of goliahs and marsupial lions on Arenes.

"I also recommend that we keep an eye out for each other," Penning said. "Talk about what you've experienced, share your emotions. I need to radio the mainland, but if anyone feels the need to offload, do come and see me."

She divided the group into teams, some to pick up their work, others to tackle the storage containers, and a small group to stand guard around the camp armed with the rifles the team possessed. Just in case.

Lette supposed she could get on with her archival research but wasn't looking forward to it. She had no idea how she'd be able to concentrate on old records with her mind's eye replaying the nightmare. The others, at least, would be working in teams, finding comfort in each other's company.

"Lette," Penning said. "Could you follow me?"

They made their way back to camp, the larger group splitting up into smaller parties.

"I could use your help, Lette," Penning said. "There'll be a lot to get organised. We'll need to radio the AFP first, then the museum. I suspect that will take a lot longer."

"Do you really think they'll shut the camp down?"

"I have no doubt about it. They'll not want to lose any other members of the team. But it'll take time to wind the camp down. For one, the police won't want to let anybody go until they've figured out that we aren't murderers. Also, the logistics are considerable. The museum will have to organise boats from Geraldton. Evacuation will have to happen in phases, I suspect. You and I will need to look at a roster, to see who can leave first and who might advance our research here by staying longer."

"With all due respect to Mr Fieldman and Bruce, but it seems a shame to depart from such a promising site."

"It is indeed, but don't forget that we've already accumulated a great many finds – which we'll have to pack,

– and uncovered enough information to be able to form a picture of what happened here. There will be plenty of work to do for us in Fremantle once we've organised our departure from Arenes. And who knows, we might be able to return some day, with adequate safety measures in place."

"Speaking of safety measures," Lette said. "I think we need to do more than just pack up the camp. I think we need to erase our presence as much as possible. Things like the car park that would be a tell-tale sign. Word of the wreck will get out at some point."

"You're absolutely right," Penning agreed, guessing where Lette was headed with her reasoning. "The last thing we need is for treasure hunters to blunder into the area. That, my girl, will be your first responsibility. Talk to the team working on the storage containers, draw up a plan. Also, with regards to packing up, we'll have to leave the Morgue intact as long as possible. The police might want to verify that all the remnants are truly historical and compare the thylacoleo carnifex teeth marks with whatever marks those animals might have left on Martin and Bruce."

Lette nodded.

"Providing that is, that you're willing to start our co-operation right here and now."

"I am," Lette said, relieved that she'd have practical matters to worry about.

The police arrived in the late afternoon, flying in on two large helicopters. A forensic team was led to ground zero to start unravelling the gory puzzle that awaited them. A detective inspector, accompanied by another detective, spoke to Penning and Lette in one of the office tents. It started as a matter-of-fact report delivered by Penning, including their discovery of goliah bones and evidence of thylacoleo carnifex teeth marks on the bones of unfortunate seventeenth century Dutchmen.

"I understand that it may sound farfetched," Penning said. "But we have the goliah bones of the animal killed in 1616 in one of our tents. As well as the corpse of the goliah that was killed yesterday. And I suspect that the tooth marks on the remnants of the Dutch crew will match those your forensic experts will find on the bodies of our unfortunate colleagues."

The two policemen exchanged a look. The detective inspector said, "We'll certainly investigate if we can substantiate your suggestion that this thylcolo…"

"Thylacoleo carnifex," Penning said. "But it might be easier to refer to it as a marsupial lion."

"A prehistoric creature, long extinct," the detective pointed out.

"That was the assumption," Penning agreed.

"Moreover," the detective said. "Whereas I understand you've got a big roo to show us, nobody actually saw this…lion last night? Other than the victims?"

"Lions," Lette said. "They live and hunt in packs. We heard more than one in the camp last night."

"Making noises that, apparently, the lyrebirds have been making as well," the detective said, raising his eyebrows.

"Well, yes," Lette conceded. "But in *imitation* of the real thing."

"Making noises that, apparently, the lyrebirds have been making as well."

(Illustration by Julieann Williams)

"They excel at realistic mimicry," the detective inspector said. "It's most remarkable."

The detective shrugged. "With all due respect, the possibility that these lyrebirds have passed this imitation from generation to generation is less far-fetched than the notion that some sort of ice-age sabretooth tiger is on a walkabout in the bush."

"Ice-age sabretooth tiger?" Penning asked, her voice a combination of disbelief and anger.

"Yeah, like in that animation movie," the detective shrugged again. "My kids love it. Come to think of it, perhaps you've seen it as well. Triggered the imagination perhaps?"

Penning was known for her acutely analytical mind and the suggestions that she was prone to fanciful imagination angered Lette enough to resort to an old Surinamese proverb, *"Kromanti taki, si na bribi,"* which meant as much as 'those who don't believe will find out the hard way'.

The detective looked annoyed. "No need for Blackie gibberish here, Missy."

"Blackie?" Lette bristled, taking a deep breath for a more detailed retort, but Penning placed a hand on her arm and gave it a light squeeze. At the same time, the detective inspector frowned.

"That comment was uncalled for, George," he admonished his colleague.

The detective looked Lette in the eye. "Soz, Missy, I didn't mean to offend."

His eyes spoke otherwise, daring her to make an issue out of it. Lette took another deep breath, reminding herself that the current power structure didn't make this an opportune time to pick a fight with this Neanderthal. Wearily, she concluded that the world was still filled with men like these and that she was probably facing a lifetime of this particular struggle. There would be others she could ask as to what century they thought they were living in.

"We are scientists, Detective," Penning said with pursed lips. "Not prone to using children's animation movies as a framework of reference. I would appreciate it if you could respect that."

"Fair dinkum," the detective inspector responded. "Now there are some other questions I'd like to ask you. Do you have any reason to believe that any of your people here had reason to dislike the victims?"

"A grudge of sorts?" the detective supplied helpfully. "Professional or personal?"

This time it was Lette and Penning who exchanged a look. One that was full of mutual understanding. It was going to be a long, long week.

28. *De Blokzeyl*

Arenes, The Southland, 1616

Their luck turned on the seventh day. Miraculously, against all odds, a shout thrilled through the air. A shout full of near hysterical relief.

"Sails! Sails ho!"

The remaining *Armuyden* survivors hastily gathered atop of the main cave, where the lookouts were setting fire to the pile of wood that had been assembled as beacon.

Leyn and Heike took longer to get there.

"Where the devil are those two? They've been gone for hours. Again!" Niklas grumbled, to frown when he saw the two emerge from one of the smaller caves, Leyn looking flustered and embarrassed, Heike dreamily content.

"Do you two really think there was nought better to do?" Niklas scolded them, as they joined the others.

"Not really," Heike answered with a sated smile.

Leyn ignored the grumbles. A whole new dimension of existence had been revealed to him during the hours that he and Heike had explored the smaller caves…and each other. It had brought him elation but also a vague sense of guilt, so he avoided meeting Niklas's eye. Instead, Leyn looked out over the sea apprehensively, recalling all too well his last two sightings of sails.

The sky was magnificently blue, clear of clouds. The ocean's swelling waves rolled in with majestic grace, powerful but devoid of menace or hostility. As smoke from the beacon drifted into the air it was greeted by a cannon shot from the ship that sailed in serenely from the south.

She had white sails, Leyn noted with relief. And a Dutch tricolour at her stern. He exclaimed, "She's a Dutchman, one of ours!"

A nearby sailor grinned. "I recognise her, she sailed out with us. She is *De Blokzeyl*. She separated from the fleet at the Cape of Good Hope."

The wounded who could emerged from the cave now to gape at the blessed sight of rescue. The two children yelled excitedly and danced around Leyn and Heike.

Leyn sighed.

Just twenty of us left alive.

De Blokzeyl anchored at a safe distance from the cliffs. The initial relief of *De Armuyden* survivors was hampered somewhat by the realisation that their would-be rescuers wouldn't be able to simply sail up to the treacherous shoreline platform, nor send boats there. How were they going to get aboard?

The captain of *De Blokzeyl* seemed to have anticipated this problem, for they saw the crew aboard the ship launch both yawl and longboat. The yawl sailed south, the longboat north.

"Looking for a suitable place to land," Niklas commented. "We're likely to face the prospect of a long walk before we can be taken off Arenes."

He immediately began giving those who were well enough instructions to start constructing makeshift stretchers to carry those who were unable to walk or wouldn't be able to get very far on their own feet.

When the stretchers were ready, most drifted back to the edge of the escarpment to gaze at *De Blokzeyl*, so near yet so unreachable. For the immediate moment, anyway.

Leyn folded an arm around Heike's shoulders, and she leant against him in response.

"It's so different just a week later, in daylight. Was it all real, Leyn?"

"I don't know, I just don't know."

"You don't know much, do you now?"

Leyn grinned. He reckoned he knew a little more than he did a week ago. He knew now that they would live a little longer, and mayhap…he looked at Heike and thought, *to die for.*

Nonetheless, he wasn't inclined to disagree, so answered honestly, "Nay, I don't know much at all."

29. Stickybeaked Sandgropers

Arenes, Western Australia, 2016

"Bloody hell, I told you they were hiding something!"

It was extreme low tide and three men, rough looking fellows, stood at the edge of the shoreline platform. The outline of a great many cannons on the seabed were clearly visible.

"Those are old shooters," the eldest of them continued speaking in a broad Aussie drawl. "Lends a lot of weight to those rumours that the museum folk found a new VOC wreck."

"Streuth! Lucky for us that one of 'em got tanked enough to start blabbing," a second man —wearing a baseball cap – grinned.

The third man, the youngest who had a rifle slung over his shoulder, looked puzzled. "You'd reckon they'd be big-noting themselves all over the media if it was another Dutchman. Get a lot of attention that way."

"Yep," the oldest man nodded. "But they sure kept this one quiet, didn't they? All that hush-hush will be for a good reason, mark my words. There's something here they don't want us to know about."

The man with the baseball cap chuckled. "Betcha they'll be as cross as a frog in a sock if they knew that us stickey-beaked Sandgropers[30] came to have a gander at the Back of Bourke[31]."

"No worries," the oldest man smirked. "We'll head back up the cliff, set up camp, grab some tucker and then tomorrow we'll come down and start fossicking around some."

"Find enough cabbage to last us all a lifetime," the man with the baseball cap predicted confidently.

When they reached the cave on the plateau, where they had parked the flatbed pick-up truck they'd rented in Maroons Cove, they were met by a surprising sight.

An animal far bigger and stockier than a large red roo, with a strange flat face, was circling the truck curiously, sniffing at their gear.

"Oi, get away from our ute!" The man with the baseball cap shouted.

Had the men been more observant, they would have noticed the goliah's juvenile curiosity, but all they saw was a pest.

"Shoot the fucker," the older man ordered the younger one.

"Can't we just chase it away?" the younger man objected.

"Pour yourself a glass of concrete, sunshine," the elder man snarled. "We're not here to fuck spiders, we got hard yakka to do and I'll be damned if I'm going to have to deal with vermin getting in our way."

---

[30] Nosy West Australians
[31] A very distant isolated location

The younger man nodded and prepared his rifle for a shot. The animal regarded him curiously, apparently entirely oblivious of the rifle's purpose.

Moments later the shot rang out, disturbing the solemn serenity around the cave. The younger man was a good marksman and the goliah was killed instantly, slumping to the ground with a surprised expression on its flat face.

In the distance, somewhere on the plains, the shot was answered by angry roars.

THE END

Acknowledgments

Brighton, England, 2025

Many thanks to Yvette Boertje whose Defragged History narration of *De Batavia* shipwreck and mutiny (Check it out on YouTube!) formed the first spark of inspiration for this story. Bethanks also to the Western Australian Museum whose thunder I have so shamelessly stolen, as anyone even vaguely familiar with *De Zuytdorp* wreck will realise when reading my fictional account of *De Armuyden's* demise.

Many thanks also to my former pupils at the *Openbare Schoolgemeenschap Bijlmer (OSB)*, who taught me what it's like to be a proud Surinamer. It's a heritage I share with them, though way back when my forefolks were, ahem, on the other side of things there. My apologies for the role my family played in Surinamese history were gracefully accepted by my OSB pupils who were intrigued by the notion that my ancestors had possibly owned theirs and mentioned gleefully that they weren't surprised I had slavedrivers in my ancestry, given my record in assigning homework. I hope Lette reflects your indomitable spirit, *mi pikin koni*. Special thanks to former pupil Vesla Vyent, who kindly helped me with Sranantongo (Sranan), the informal language of Surinam also used in Lette's Bijlmer.

Special thanks also need to go Down Under, to Heather Santilli who kindly discussed Bruce with me, and Julieann Williams who advised me to acknowledge the importance of the Indigenous people of Australia as original owners of the land and guardians of its legacy. She also delved into the Pleistocene period with me to explore the story potential of some of its denizens. Sorry that the giant Wombats didn't make it in, maybe next time! Last, but certainly not least, we discussed the potential of local feathered friends and fiends, which Julieann then kindly offered to illustrate.

Back in Sussex, many thanks also to James Murphy for providing feedback and Julie Gorringe who advised on a very early version of this story and was happy to donate one of her images of 'Dirty' Dick Trucker to the book. I dursn't forget Tom Brown, the cover artist who designed and made the covers for the Flying Dutchman Trilogy and agreed to make one for *Rousing the Duvelsbeest* so that some consistency could be maintained (*Duvelsbeest* is a distant cousin of the Trilogy and there is some overlap). If you're interested in Tom's work, you can find him at: https://mothfestival.wordpress.com/commissioning-tom/.

Tom also provided many of the interior illustrations.

My German is very poor indeed and I have no idea if the phrases I used were in (similar) usage in the 17th century. I wasn't trying to be accurate there, just liked the idea of Heike uttering the occasional phrase in her mother tongue.

The procoptodon goliahs and thylacoleo carnifexes inhabited large swathes of the Australian continent during the Pleistocene and their extant existence overlapped with that of the Indigenous people, as reflected in their histories and rock art. I cannot even begin to fathom the courage required to interact with such creatures, so once again, all my respect.

The ability of the marsupial lions in *Rousing the Duvelsbeest* to be sentient and omniscient enough to differentiate between good and evil is highly debatable, of course. In fact, it had a notably smaller brain than contemporary predatory cats its size because so much space was required for the musculature needed for that insane biting power. Then again, animals do sometimes tend to perceive certain human characteristics and, as you have discovered, anything is possible on Arenes.

If you would like to sample more of my historical fiction in a similar vein, do try *The Flying Dutchman Book 1: Bleak Future*, which features Peter and Liselotte Haelen. I'm currently close to completing the first draft of the second book in this trilogy: *Malign Shadows*. Niklas Zonvelt is present throughout *Malign Shadows* as important secondary character and does indeed introduce Liselotte to Leyn and Heike in Amboyna. Steyn Florentin also makes an appearance, as do *De Blokzeyl* and *De Christine*. I hope to see Malign Shadows published somewhere in 2026.

Fair winds to you.

Nils Visser
January 19th, 2025, Brighton, England.

If you enjoyed this novella, why not try the author's novel *The Flying Dutchman: Bleak Future*? There are two professionally narrated chapters available on YouTube as free sample in which you can meet Liselotte Haelen (search for The Drowned Land of Reimerswaal), or else just dive straight in by getting the gorgeously illustrated paperback or the e-book (without the illustrations). Available at all online retailers.

www.ingramcontent.com/pod-product-compliance
Lightning Source LLC
Chambersburg PA
CBHW032011180726
48283CB00008B/2627